"Have dinner with me."

Quinn's deep voice sounded much too close to her ear, his breath ghosting over her cheek.

Abigail shivered, muscles clenching low in her abdomen. Carefully, she turned her head and her gaze met his. His gray eyes were pewter-dark and warm. The faint scent of male cologne reached her as he leaned closer, seeming to loom larger, blocking out the rest of the room. Heat washed over her.

She struggled to form a reply. Her senses urged her to lean forward, bury her face against his throat and breathe in that elusive male scent that seemed to be his alone.

"Come with me, Abby." His deep drawl was mesmerizing. "You know you want to."

Abby stared, fascinated by the darkening of his gray eyes and the awareness that felt as if a web were spun between them, heating the air separating them and pulling her closer.

Oh, no, she thought with sudden clarity. I am in *such* trouble with you, Quinn.

D0451504

Dear Reader,

I was delighted when I was asked to be a part of Harlequin's sixtieth anniversary celebration by participating in the FAMOUS FAMILIES promotion for the Silhouette Special Edition line. I loved writing the original four McCLOUDS OF MONTANA books and had just as much fun with this fifth book.

Quinn McCloud grew up far from Montana, and his cousins in Wolf Creek don't know he exists—but he's known about them for some time. He's wary of family ties when he arrives in Wolf Creek—at least, until he meets lovely, sharp-tongued and sexy Abigail Foster. Soon, she has him wondering whether acknowledging his connection to the powerful McCloud clan might be a good thing. Falling in love with Abigail is inevitable but Quinn questions whether he can cease his wandering and stay in Wolf Creek forever. Abigail, however, can accept no less from the man she loves.

I hope you enjoy Abigail and Quinn's story as much as I did—happy reading!

Warmly,

Lois

QUINN McCLOUD'S CHRISTMAS BRIDE

LOIS FAYE DYER

SPECIAL EDITION®

Published by Silhouette Books

America's Publisher of Contemporary Romance

If you purchased this book without a cover you should be aware that this book is stolen property. It was reported as "unsold and destroyed" to the publisher, and neither the author nor the publisher has received any payment for this "stripped book."

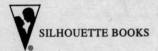

SILHOUETTE BOOKS

ISBN-13: 978-0-373-65489-5

Recycling programs for this product may not exist in your area.

QUINN McCLOUD'S CHRISTMAS BRIDE

Copyright © 2009 by Lois Faye Dyer

All rights reserved. Except for use in any review, the reproduction or utilization of this work in whole or in part in any form by any electronic, mechanical or other means, now known or hereafter invented, including xerography, photocopying and recording, or in any information storage or retrieval system, is forbidden without the written permission of the editorial office, Silhouette Books, 233 Broadway, New York, NY 10279 U.S.A.

This is a work of fiction. Names, characters, places and incidents are either the product of the author's imagination or are used fictitiously, and any resemblance to actual persons, living or dead, business establishments, events or locales is entirely coincidental.

This edition published by arrangement with Harlequin Books S.A.

® and TM are trademarks of Harlequin Books S.A., used under license. Trademarks indicated with ® are registered in the United States Patent and Trademark Office, the Canadian Trade Marks Office and in other countries.

Visit Silhouette Books at www.eHarlequin.com

Printed in U.S.A.

Books by Lois Faye Dyer

Silhouette Special Edition

Lonesome Cowboy #1038
He's Got His Daddy's Eyes #1129
The Cowboy Takes a Wife #1198
The Only Cowboy for Caitlin #1253
Cattleman's Courtship #1306
Cattleman's Bride-to-Be #1457
Practice Makes Pregnant #1569
Cattleman's Heart #1605
The Prince's Bride #1640
*Luke's Proposal #1745
*Jesse's Child #1776
*Chase's Promise #1791
*Trey's Secret #1823
**The Princess and the Cowboy #1865
†Triple Trouble #1957
*Quinn McCloud's Christmas Bride #2007

*The McClouds of Montana
**The Hunt for Cinderella
†Fortunes of Texas: Return to Red Rock

LOIS FAYE DYER

lives in a small town on the shore of beautiful Puget Sound in the Pacific Northwest with her two eccentric and lovable cats, Chloe and Evie. She loves to hear from readers and you can write to her c/o Paperbacks Plus, 1618 Bay Street, Port Orchard, WA 98366. Visit her on the Web at www.LoisDyer.com.

For all my readers who told me they loved the McClouds
and hated to see their story end…

Chapter One

Wolf Creek, Montana
Mid-September

"Aunt Natasha? Aunt Elizabeth?"

Abigail Foster donned a light sweater and stepped out onto the wide porch, letting the screen door slap shut behind her. Two wicker chairs were pushed back from the white table in the far corner of the porch. An enameled tray and a plate with several sugar cookies sat next to a Wedgwood teapot atop the blue cloth. Lemon slices floated on the surface of amber-colored tea in delicate blue and white cups. Her aunts had obviously been interrupted during their afternoon Earl Grey break and had left the comfortable corner, sheltered by the potato vine that climbed up the trellis.

But where had they gone? Abigail looked up and down the wide street. Down the block, two eight-year-olds rode bicycles, weaving in and out of the autumn leaves collecting in red and gold drifts in the gutters. Two joggers, accompanied by a cocker spaniel tugging on his leash, circled around the boys and kept on going. The rhythm of the neighborhood ticked on as usual. But Abigail didn't see her great-aunts.

She crossed the porch and descended the broad, white-painted steps, following the brick walkway around the house to the side yard. She heard the murmur of voices as she neared the back of the house. The rumble of a deeper, male voice mingled with her aunts' lighter tones had her quickening her steps.

Leaves crunched under her boots as she rounded the corner of the house. She made a mental note to clear the fallen leaves from the bed of chrysanthemums and dahlias edging the white clapboard siding over the next day or two. She knew from experience that the lovely Indian summer days would quickly turn to chillier October weeks, followed by snow in November.

The voices grew louder as she reached the backyard. A silver-gray pickup truck was parked on the gravel drive off the alleyway, just next to the stairs that climbed up the outside wall of the garage to the second-floor apartment above.

A tall man, dressed in faded jeans and boots with a blue flannel shirt stretched across broad shoulders, stood with his back to her, talking to her aunts. A big yellow dog nosed the leaves at their feet.

The dog raised his head, saw her, barked and charged.

Startled, Abigail froze, her eyes widening. The dog was huge and the closer he drew, the bigger and scarier he seemed.

"Buddy. Down." The deep male voice was sharp, the command undeniable.

The dog halted in midcharge and dropped to the ground.

Abigail stared at him. As her racing heartbeat slowed to something approaching normal, she realized that what she'd thought was a fierce predator was actually a blond Labrador retriever. He panted, his pink tongue lolling while his big brown eyes fixed on her with eager friendliness. His ears lifted with endearing interest as he eyed her.

"Sorry, ma'am."

Abigail looked up. The man walked toward the dog, pausing when he reached him. He limped slightly, she noted, but somehow, it didn't dilute the sheer power he projected. His coal-black hair was cut short. Equally dark eyebrows arched above gray eyes, startlingly pale in his suntanned face.

"Buddy's friendly—he wouldn't hurt you." He

grinned, the twinkle in his eye disarming, and the flash of white teeth and easy quirk of his lips told her this was a man accustomed to charming women.

Alarm bells went off. The last time a man had smiled at her with that level of male interest and charm was during her senior year at college and things hadn't ended well. The whirlwind relationship and six-month marriage that followed had taught her a lesson about charming men she'd never forget. She was immediately suspicious of the dog owner's motives.

"Really?" she said coolly, lifting an eyebrow in disbelief. "He has an impressive set of teeth. He's never bitten anyone?"

"No, ma'am," he responded solemnly, although his eyes reflected amusement. "Not unless I told him to."

Despite herself, Abigail gaped. "You *tell* him to bite people?"

"Only criminals—and only in the line of duty," he amended.

Oh, no. Abigail nearly groaned aloud. Surely he wasn't…

"This is Mr. McCloud, Abigail," Natasha said as she and her sister, Elizabeth, joined them. "He's from the Colter Investigation Agency in Seattle. He'll be our acting sheriff until the town council can hire someone permanent."

"I see." Abigail eyed him with curiosity. "It's quite a coincidence that you work for Ren Colter's agency. A local rancher, Chase McCloud, is his business partner. Are you related to Chase?"

"I'd never met Chase before I went to work there," Quinn said with a slight smile. "I knew Ren—we met while working on a project overseas." He shrugged. "When he heard I was looking to change jobs, he offered me a spot in Seattle. That's where I met Chase."

"I suppose that only proves we live in a small world." Curiosity satisfied, Abigail belatedly remembered her manners and held out her hand. "Welcome to Wolf Creek, Mr. McCloud."

"Call me Quinn," he said easily, taking her hand in his. "Mr. McCloud is too formal."

His hand was warm, the palm and fingers slightly rough beneath hers. A working man's hand, she thought, wondering what it was about a lawman's work that created calluses. Too aware of the latent strength in his grip, she drew her hand from his.

She didn't think she'd ever seen eyes quite like his— pale gray irises rimmed with black—and his eyelashes were as dark as his hair and brows in his suntanned face. Belatedly, she realized she was staring and forced her gaze away from him. She glanced at the silver truck parked next to the garage, noted the black tarp covering bulky, unidentifiable shapes in the pickup bed and looked back at him. "You're staying in the apartment?"

He nodded. "Ren told me the mayor made arrangements for me to rent it from your aunts."

"We must have forgotten to mention it, dear." Natasha gave her a guileless smile.

Abigail sighed with resignation. Elizabeth and Natasha were seventy-five and seventy-seven, and their minds were as spry as their wiry bodies. It was far more likely her aunts had volunteered the apartment as soon as they discovered that the late Sheriff Adams's replacement was a single male.

He'd turned his attention away from her, listening attentively as Elizabeth asked him whether he'd had a good trip. Abigail took advantage of his distraction and lowered her lashes, screening her eyes, her gaze dropping to his hands.

Just as she thought, the ring finger of his left hand was bare.

Her aunts meant well, but Abigail really wished they'd stop trying to find a man for her.

"…wouldn't we, Abigail?"

"Hmm?" While she'd been frowning at Quinn McCloud's ringless left hand and pondering her aunts' possible matchmaking, Elizabeth had apparently made a comment that required her agreement. About something.

"I was telling Mr. McCloud we would be delighted to have him join us for dinner." Elizabeth eyed her with a faint frown, clearly wondering why her great-niece was woolgathering when good manners dictated she pay attention to the conversation.

"Of course." Abigail forced a smile. Why Quinn

McCloud's handsome face, amused gray eyes and half grin raised her hackles to the extent they did, she didn't know. She did know, however, that she found it distinctly annoying that her aunts apparently thought he was charming.

The wry look he gave her told her he knew she wouldn't have offered the invitation if it had been her choice.

"That's very nice of you all, but I'll have to take a rain check," he said. "I need to unload the truck and check in at the office."

"Of course." Elizabeth was clearly disappointed, but then she brightened. "The Chamber of Commerce is holding a meet-and-greet hour later this week to introduce you to everyone. I'm sure we'll see you there. And of course," she added, "we'll see you often, I'm sure, since you'll be living only a few steps across our backyard."

"The apartment is fully furnished with towels and linens," Natasha chimed in with a smile. "but if there's anything you need, don't hesitate to knock on our door. I'm sure Abigail will be happy to help you."

It was all Abigail could do to keep from rolling her eyes. "Everyone is grateful you could step in on such short notice. I'm sure we'll all do what we can to make sure you're comfortable while you're here."

"I appreciate it. Now, if you ladies will excuse me, I'd better unload the truck."

"Certainly," Natasha and Elizabeth said in near unison.

He snapped his fingers and the big yellow Lab

jumped to his feet, following him when he nodded at the three women and walked away.

Elizabeth and Natasha looked after him with pleased expressions.

Abigail refused to watch him. She spun on her heel and walked purposefully toward the back porch of the big Victorian house she and her aunts called home. Marching up the steps, she pulled open the screen door and stepped inside, her boots echoing on the wooden boards as she crossed the porch and entered the house.

The sunny old-fashioned kitchen was large and square, with a pantry opening off one side. Abigail collected the teakettle from the stove, filled it at the tap and returned to set it on the burner. She switched on the heat beneath the kettle with a snap and marched to the cupboard to take down a rose-and-white teapot with three matching cups and saucers.

Why the prospect of Quinn McCloud living in the apartment above the garage was such an irritant, she didn't know. *Some things,* she thought as she opened a drawer to take out three teaspoons and butter knives, *defied simple explanation.* There was simply something about him that shrieked "trouble."

And that's sufficient reason to be wary, she told herself as she carried a tray with a plate of pumpkin-spice bread, the silverware, a covered butter dish and three small plates through the living room. She deposited them on the front porch's wicker table and returned to the kitchen with the now-cold Wedgwood pot and cups just as her great-aunts bustled through the back door.

"Such a nice young man," Elizabeth declared.

"Yes, very," Natasha agreed. Beneath her short white curls, her eyes sparkled. "Don't you think so, Abigail?"

"I don't know him well enough to make a judgment," Abigail replied. The kettle whistled and she poured boiling water into the rose-and-white teapot. "I thought you might want to join me since your earlier tea was interrupted?"

She picked up the tray with the fresh pot and three matching cups and delicate saucers, catching the quick glance her great-aunts exchanged before she left the kitchen.

Certain they'd follow, she walked through the living room and out onto the wide porch, settling the tray atop the wicker table. By the time she'd unloaded the dishes Natasha and Elizabeth joined her. For the next few moments, the three were occupied with the stirring of sugar into cups and buttering of slices of rich golden brown sweetbread.

"It's wonderful timing to have a renter for the apartment, just when we need a bit of extra cash for new snow tires and furnace maintenance before winter arrives," Elizabeth said.

Abigail murmured a noncommittal agreement, sipping her tea.

"And Mr. McCloud seems like a very nice young man," Natasha responded, giving Abigail a sideways glance.

"Mmm," Abigail responded, popping a bite of bread into her mouth to avoid answering. She'd read the résumé sent by Colter Investigations to the town council when they'd requested a temporary replacement after a heart attack felled Sheriff Adams. "Nice young man" weren't exactly the words she would have used to describe someone who'd spent most of his adult life in violent action around the world. Perhaps "mercenary" might fit, she thought.

Elizabeth peered at her over the rims of her glasses, her deep blue eyes mirrors of Abigail's thick-lashed ones. "You don't seem impressed by Mr. McCloud, Abigail," she said bluntly. "Why not?"

Abigail chewed, swallowed and took a sip of tea. "Because," she said, returning the delicate china cup to its saucer. She thought about telling her great-aunt her objection was to Quinn McCloud's work history. But since Elizabeth was a member of the town council and had read the same résumé, she opted for a different tack. "He's too handsome," Abigail modified.

"How on earth can a man be too handsome?" Natasha put in with astonishment. "That's like saying someone's too rich or a woman is too pretty—it's just not possible."

"And he's too charming," Abigail added.

Elizabeth rolled her eyes. "Regardless, that doesn't mean Mr. McCloud isn't a nice man. I want you to promise you'll give him a chance before making up your mind to dislike him."

Abigail crossed the fingers of her left hand, out of her aunts' sight on her lap. "I promise."

Quinn reached his truck and looked over his shoulder just in time to see Abigail march up the back steps. The mid-afternoon sunlight burnished her dark brown hair, pulled up in a ponytail that swung smartly from side to side with each step she took. Faded jeans fit snugly over the lush curve of her bottom and down her long legs. She wore black rubber gardening boots on her feet and the bright red sweater covered a plain white T-shirt. She pulled open the screen door and disappeared inside, the door slapping shut with a definite smack of finality.

The two older ladies followed her more slowly, heads together as they whispered.

He grinned and shook his head. The great-aunts seemed glad to have him living over their garage, but for some reason, Miss Abigail had disliked him on sight.

Which sure as hell wasn't how he felt about her, he thought. There wasn't anything overtly sexual about Abigail Foster, but for some reason, she turned him on. He could swear she wasn't wearing a lick of makeup— her face looked fresh scrubbed, her lips naturally pink. She had a small straight nose above a lush mouth with a plump lower lip, deep blue eyes edged with thick dark lashes below equally etched eyebrows. Her skin was fair, with a dusting of tiny freckles over the arch of her cheekbones. And her chin had a distinctly stubborn set, especially when she looked at him and her eyes narrowed with suspicion.

He walked around the pickup, untying knots as he went and freeing the nylon rope holding the tarp in place.

What was it Ren's agency report had said about the Fosters? He thought for a moment as he yanked the rope free and tossed the tarp back.

Oh, yeah. She's a librarian. And one of her aunts—great-aunts, he corrected himself—was the town librarian before Abigail took over.

Quinn lowered the pickup's tailgate and grabbed his duffel bag in one hand, a large bag of dry dog food with his other.

"Come on, Buddy," he called. The dog immediately left his inspection of the base of a nearby maple tree and followed him up the stairs to the landing, bounding inside when Quinn unlocked and shoved open the door.

Just as he stepped over the threshold, a breeze carried the faint sound of feminine voices from the front of the house.

He grinned. Wolf Creek might not offer the excitement of his last case, but after meeting Abigail and her aunts, life suddenly looked much more interesting.

Which was more than he'd hoped for when he took this job. Only four days ago he'd been staring out the window of his Belltown apartment in Seattle, watching rain pelt down while the wind sent a flurry of leaves spinning by.

He wasn't fully recuperated from his last assignment for Colter Investigations. Executing the plan to recover a client's stolen yacht had ended with surgery to remove a bullet from his left thigh. He'd been gloomily contemplating the likelihood of another month or two spent in physical therapy, lifting weights with the rainy Seattle weather outside his window.

A chance to escape the gray rain was only part of the reason he'd accepted when his boss, Ren Colter, phoned with an offer of a temporary job as sheriff of Wolf Creek, Montana.

Quinn also decided it was a good opportunity to check out his uncle and cousins without them knowing he was doing so.

He was eighteen years old when he'd discovered he had an uncle, John McCloud, who lived and ranched near Wolf Creek. That was the year Quinn went to court and gained permission to open his adoption file. He'd never gotten along with his mother's husband, who'd legally adopted him when he was a baby. In fact, Quinn had left home in Texas at sixteen and taken a job on a ranch in New Mexico. At eighteen, before joining the military, he wanted to learn his biological father's name—Sean McCloud—so he could legally change his own surname to match.

It was several years later, though, before he had time to browse the Internet and locate information on his father's family.

But he doubted John McCloud knew he existed. His mother hadn't married Sean McCloud and Quinn was born after his father died. Quinn was born in a small town in Texas while Sean died at a rodeo in Mexico. Even if his uncle knew his brother had impregnated a young woman, Quinn doubted there was any way to trace either his mother or himself.

He'd never felt any urgency to visit Wolf Creek and introduce himself. He had no brothers or sisters and the connection between him and his mother was thin, with the occasional phone call every few years. She hadn't been the least bit maternal. Quinn didn't spend time thinking about it, but if asked, would probably shrug off the concept of family. He'd never had one. And logically speaking, his observations told him the obligations far outweighed the benefits.

It was a measure of his boredom at being sidelined in rainy Seattle that he'd decided the opportunity to fill in for the sheriff might also be a good time to check out the McClouds.

So here he was, he thought, quickly assessing the comfortable living room. There was a small utility kitchen at one end of the room and he carried Buddy's bag of dog food there, dropping it on the floor by the counter.

The Lab whined, nosing the bag and looking hopefully up at Quinn.

"All right, all right. I guess you deserve a treat after

being cooped up in the truck for two long days." He ruffled the dog's silky ears.

It only took moments to fill a bowl with food and set it on the floor. Buddy promptly buried his nose in the bowl, tail wagging with enthusiasm.

Quinn took a glass from the cupboard and filled it from the tap, drinking water while looking out the window. The back door of the Foster house opened and Abigail stepped out. His gaze followed the lift of her arms as she shook out a small rug, the move stretching her red sweater snug across the curve of her breasts. She gave the rug a last shake, tossed it over one arm, and disappeared inside the house once more.

Oh, yeah, he thought with a smile of anticipation. *Living across the lawn from Abigail Foster held definite possibilities.*

Chapter Two

That evening, Abigail left her aunts watching the ten o'clock news in the living room and headed upstairs. Her bedroom was at the back of the house, with tall sashed windows overlooking the back lawn, the flower beds, the big oak tree in the far corner, the garage and alley. She glanced out the window; the gravel parking slot was empty and the garage apartment windows were dark.

Annoyed with herself when she realized she was curious to see if Quinn had returned from his outing, she purposely turned her back on the view. Collecting pajamas from the old-fashioned cherrywood dresser that matched her four-poster bed, she left the bedroom for the bathroom down the hall.

By ten-thirty, Abigail was settled in bed, pillows at her back, reading. This was one of her favorite times of the day. Although she was surrounded by books five days a week, eight hours a day at the library, she relished the quiet hour or two she had each night to read in the comfortable surroundings of her bedroom.

Engrossed in a new historical mystery from one of her favorite authors, she looked up to murmur an absent-minded reply when her aunts walked by her door and said good-night. When she reluctantly tucked a bookmark between the pages and set the novel aside, her bedside clock read ten minutes after midnight.

She snapped off the lamp on the nightstand, only then realizing she'd forgotten to open the window. Tossing back the covers, she hurried across the braided rug that covered the center of the floor, the polished hardwood cold beneath her bare toes when she stepped off at the edge. As she unlatched the window and pushed it upward, she noticed Quinn's silver pickup was again parked next to the garage and the apartment windows glowed with light above.

So he's back, she thought. *I wonder where he's been? Surely he wasn't working until midnight on his very first day in town?*

The drapes weren't drawn over the apartment's sliding glass doors. Past the small balcony, she could see into the main living space, a combination of kitchen/dining/living room. Quinn's dog ambled into view, followed a moment later by Quinn himself.

He wore only low-slung jeans, his torso bare. He followed the dog into the kitchen, muscles bunching and shifting as he reached to take down a bowl from a cabinet, filled it with water and bent to set it on the floor. Light gleamed over glossy black hair and supple tanned skin.

Abigail stood transfixed, staring at the scene in the apartment across the way. Quinn crossed the living space and moved out of her view. The light flicked off, the square expanse of the sliding glass doors going dark.

A breeze carried a small gust of cold air through the slightly open window and Abigail shivered. She realized she was holding her breath and audibly gasped, drawing in chilly air. Hurrying across the room, she dived back into bed, snuggling beneath the warm covers. Her feet and hands were icy but her heart hammered, her cheeks flushed with heat.

There was something so essentially male about Quinn McCloud. Despite knowing he was most likely far too handsome for his own good, or hers, either, for that matter, she was still drawn to him. She might tell her aunts she wasn't attracted to him, but she couldn't lie to herself.

He was a walking, talking, embodiment of male sex appeal. And she certainly wasn't immune to it—whatever he had, she wanted.

Not intellectually, of course, because any smart woman knew better than to be mesmerized by all that male charm and in-your-face testosterone.

But physically, Abigail bemoaned, she was as susceptible as probably every other woman who met him.

She groaned and rolled over, resolutely closing her eyes. She was determined not to think about that view of Quinn, shirtless, walking through the lamplit rooms of the apartment over her garage. So close. Barely yards away—separated from her only by the expanse of grassy backyard.

Quinn was only here as a temporary replacement. As soon as a permanent sheriff was chosen, he'd leave Wolf Creek. In the meantime, she refused to let him disturb her well-ordered life.

Her vow lasted until seven-thirty the next morning.

Dressed for work but still in her slippers, Abigail was in the kitchen, sipping her second mug of coffee for the day and packing her lunch. She heard the sound of a door closing and looked out the window over the kitchen sink to see Buddy race down the stairs from the apartment and into the backyard. He moved out of sight and she returned to cutting an apple and tucking the slices into a sandwich bag.

When she glanced up again, a smile curved her lips as she watched the big dog gambol like a puppy, nose to the ground as he tunneled through a pile of leaves before he dropped and rolled over and over, scattering them.

Like a child, she thought with amusement.

She turned away to fetch a carton of yogurt from the refrigerator and when she returned to the sink to glance out the window once more, Buddy was gone.

A moment later, however, she heard a scratching sound at the back door, followed by a bark.

When she pulled open the door, she found Buddy sitting on the back step, grinning up at her. "Well, hello, there. Would you like to come in?"

He wagged his tail and Abigail could have sworn he understood her words.

"Well, then…" She stepped back, holding the door open, and he padded into the porch, waiting politely for her to close the door and return to the kitchen. He followed her, nosing her toes inside her pink slippers, then sniffing the floor at her feet before investigating the perimeters of the kitchen. When he pushed the pantry door open, however, Abigail stopped him.

"Oh, no, you don't, not in there." She pulled the door closed and he happily followed her back to the sink.

"Have you had breakfast?" she asked. His ears perked up, his head tilted to one side and he eyed her with interest.

"How about some toast?"

He responded by planting his bottom on the floor and panting, seeming to grin at her with approval while his tail swept back and forth over the floor tiles.

Abigail burst out laughing. "I can't believe I'm

carrying on a conversation with a dog." Shaking her head at her own silliness, nevertheless she popped two slices of Elizabeth's homemade brown bread in the toaster and took down two plates and the butter.

Five minutes later, toast properly buttered, she tore Buddy's piece into quarters and put them on a plate, then bent to set the plate on the floor in front of him.

A knock sounded on the back door. Buddy's ears lifted and he gave the plate holding his toast a longing look before he loped to the door.

Given Buddy's response, Abigail was certain it must be Quinn who knocked. She opened the door, barely letting her gaze skim over him before glancing down as Buddy nudged past her to greet him. That one quick glance was enough to make her shiver with awareness.

"Buddy, what are you doing here?" Quinn sounded exasperated but resigned. "I'm sorry. I should have warned you about him. He's always curious and thinks every house is his to investigate."

"Don't apologize," Abigail said. "He's just being neighborly. In fact—" she stroked her hand over the silky crown of the dog's head "—we were just about to have breakfast."

Quinn lifted an eyebrow and eyed her, his mouth curving in a smile loaded with male interest. "Really? What's he eating?"

"Toast. Made from my aunt Elizabeth's excellent, very healthy, homemade brown bread." She refused to react to the heat that warmed her face. She rarely blushed. That Quinn could make her flush with just a look was disconcerting.

Buddy whined and looked up at her. Abigail laughed at his very human expression of appeal.

"I think he's telling me he'd like to eat it." She looked back at Quinn. "Is he allowed to have toast? Should I have asked you first?"

"He can have toast."

"Great." She stepped back and waved the two into the kitchen. "Come in—have you had breakfast? Would you like a coffee?"

"I'd kill for coffee," he told her with dead seriousness. "I didn't stop at the grocery store last night—haven't had any caffeine this morning. I think I'm going through withdrawal."

"Let me guess," she said as she crossed to the cabinet and took down a mug. "You're a person who fills the coffeemaker the night before, sets the timer and pouring a mug is the first thing you do after you get up in the morning."

"Guilty as charged. How did you guess?"

"Probably because I recognized the desperation in your voice," she said dryly. "And because that's what I do." She turned, steaming mug in hand, and faltered. Quinn leaned his hips against the counter; his dark hair gleamed as if still damp from the shower, his jaw clean shaven. He wore a brown leather bomber jacket over a button-up pale blue shirt. A black leather belt with a silver buckle threaded through the belt loops of Levi jeans and polished black cowboy boots covered his feet.

Abigail drew a breath and forced her feet to move. He pushed away from the counter and met her halfway, taking the hot mug from her. Their fingers brushed, his warm and hard against hers for one brief moment. Then he lifted the mug, sipped and sighed.

His eyes opened and he smiled at her, open, friendly, genuinely appreciative, and she couldn't keep from smiling back. In that moment of camaraderie, Quinn nudged past her defenses and she felt her heart take a direct hit.

In full retreat, she turned on her heel and walked to the sink to collect her own mug. By the time she'd filled it, her defenses were shored up once again and she faced him with equanimity.

"Would you like some toast with your coffee?"

He looked at his watch. "Much as I'd like to, I'm afraid I've got to take off. Don't want to be late my first day on the job."

"Of course." She waved a hand at his attire. "No uniform?"

"Nope."

"I'm surprised—our last sheriff wanted to wear a sports coat and tie, but the town council refused outright. They insisted he wear the same uniform as the deputies."

Quinn's lips quirked. "We negotiated—I don't have to

wear a uniform and they're not responsible for replacing any clothing destroyed or damaged in the line of duty."

"I see." Abigail thought she'd unintentionally asked about a touchy issue. "What about a gun—are you carrying a county-issued weapon?"

"I'm using my own." He flipped back his coat and she saw the leather shoulder holster with its dull black weapon. "You seem familiar with the situation—I'm guessing you must be a member of the town council?"

"No." Abigail shook her head. "Aunt Elizabeth is."

"Ah." He nodded. "Good to know." He carried his cup to the sink, rinsed it and placed it upside down on the draining rack. "Thanks for the coffee." He gave her another slow grin, walked to the door and pulled it open. "Can I give you a lift downtown?"

"No, thank you," she replied. "The library doesn't open until ten."

"Then I'll say goodbye." He snapped his fingers at Buddy and the dog loped out the door ahead of him. "Have a good day, Abby."

The way he drawled out her name, accompanied by the flash of heat in his eyes when he swept her, head-to-toe, with a slow glance, sent a shiver up her spine.

"Goodbye." She didn't add his name, unwilling to call him Quinn and knowing he'd argue if she called him Mr. McCloud.

The door closed on his back and Abigail leaned against the counter behind her for support. Once again, her heart was racing too fast and her face felt flushed after talking with him.

She fervently hoped he hadn't noticed. It was one thing for *her* to know he disturbed her in a very basic, primal way. It was another thing entirely to contemplate *him* knowing just how he affected her.

An hour later, at precisely twenty minutes before 9:00 a.m., Quinn leaned against the counter in the reception area of the sheriff's office. He cradled a steaming mug of coffee in one hand, relieved that the office break room was stocked with a decent brand. Evidently, the late sheriff had been a coffee lover, too. Outside the big plate-glass window, the occasional pickup or car drove past on Main Street. Directly across the street was the town's Carnegie library with round Greek columns and carved door arches. The early 1900s building wasn't particularly large, but the design gave it the appearance of solid character and permanence.

A woman turned the corner at the end of the block and walked briskly down the sidewalk. Quinn tensed, recognizing Abigail Foster's quick, graceful stride.

The strap of a stylish, black-and-red backpack was slung over her shoulder. She wore the same slim black slacks he'd seen her in at her house earlier, but now her feet were covered with black boots and she'd buttoned a bright red jacket over her white shirt. Her hair fell to her shoulders in a glossy sable mane, curving under to brush against the shoulders of the red jacket. Quinn knew she wore gold hoop earrings—he'd noticed earlier when they gleamed against the darkness of her hair, drawing attention to the delicate, feminine curve of her ears.

And she was dead wrong, Quinn thought, if she believed the plain white, long-sleeved shirt, buttoned up the front to just below her collarbones, was utilitarian and businesslike. As he watched her sip coffee earlier this morning, his fingers had itched to slip the buttons free and slide the shirt from her shoulders. He'd be willing to bet that the full curve of her breasts under the plain white cotton was all Abby, with no padding added.

"Do you want to read the report on the break-in last night before I officially file it, Quinn? Just in case you want to add anything?"

Deputy Karl Andersen's question interrupted Quinn's absorbed study of Abigail.

"Sure." Quinn forced his attention away from Abigail Foster.

The deputy left his desk in the corner and walked to the counter, sliding the paper-clipped sheets across the Formica surface to Quinn.

Quinn glanced out the window once again, distracted by the sway of Abby's hips as she climbed the steps to the library entrance. She paused to unlock the double doors before she pulled one open and disappeared inside.

Karl glanced at the big clock mounted on the wall

behind the counter. "There goes Abigail. You can set your watch by her—unlocks the doors by a quarter to nine every morning, locks them up again at ten minutes after five, Monday through Friday."

"What about Saturday?" Quinn asked, idly making conversation while he contemplated the feminine curves under plain black slacks and white shirt. Why he found her so compelling was a mystery since he doubted Abby purposely dressed to gain male attention. Nevertheless, she was irresistible.

"The library's only open from noon to four on Saturday," Karl said. "The library board has volunteers that work on the weekend, but I hear Abigail's usually there, too."

"Interesting lady," Quinn murmured.

"Who, Abigail?" Karl sounded surprised.

His attention caught, Quinn looked at the deputy. "You don't think so?"

"Well, she's pretty enough," Karl agreed. "But she's about the stubbornest woman I've ever known—not to mention too damned smart. Her and those great-aunts of hers are downright scary."

"Is that right?" Quinn asked, encouraging the deputy to continue talking.

"Oh, yeah." Karl nodded with conviction. "Abigail and I were in the same class from kindergarten through high school. She was valedictorian at graduation and went off to college on a full scholarship—I heard she graduated magna cum laude. I never thought she'd come back to Wolf Creek—figured she'd go off to a big city somewhere, maybe end up president of a corporation someday. But she came home and here she's stayed."

"And she took over running the library when her aunt retired?"

"Yeah. She always did love that place." Karl shook his head. "And she seems set on being married to it, just like her aunt Elizabeth. Folks in the county pretty much figure she'll end up like her two great-aunts, with no husband and no kids. Don't get me wrong," he added hastily. "She's a great person. There's nobody who's quicker to offer help if a neighbor needs anything." Karl shook his head. "No question about it, Abigail's a good woman, but she's too damned intimidating for the men in Wolf Creek. Can't imagine anyone brave enough, or smart enough, to go toe-to-toe with Abigail Foster and win."

Quinn laughed out loud. "She doesn't look like she could shoot a man down at twenty paces."

"Ha." Karl's voice held conviction. "Just try making a pass at her. You'll find out soon enough. She doesn't need a gun—she can strip hide off a man with her tongue."

"Huh. Sounds like quite a challenge," Quinn commented, picking up the report. He wasn't convinced Karl's analysis of Abby and her great-aunts was accurate. Granted, he was new to town and Karl had lived here all his life. But sometimes familiarity didn't necessarily equal understanding. Until he spent more time with Abby, he'd reserve judgment. And spending time with Abby was looking more and more interesting, he thought with amusement.

"Do you have any guesses as to who's behind the breaking and entering last night?" he said aloud, skimming the deputy's case notes.

"Not a clue." Karl frowned, running his hand over his military buzz cut hair. "Probably a bunch of kids with too much time on their hands and a couple cans of beer to make them brave."

Quinn looked up. "Does that happen often in Wolf Creek?"

"Often enough." Karl shrugged. "You know what teenagers are like. I remember painting the town's water tower pink and green when I was fifteen."

"Girl colors," Quinn said with a grin.

"Yeah, we couldn't find any black." Karl's answering grin was rueful. "A skull-and-crossbones painted in green and pink didn't make the statement of rebellion we were aiming for."

"I'm guessing you were caught?"

"Oh, yeah. Our dads made us repaint the whole tower. And we had to buy the white paint, too. I worked half the summer, stacking hay bales on the McCloud Ranch, to earn enough money to pay for the paint."

It was a perfect opening to ask the talkative deputy about the McCloud family, but Quinn let the subject drop. He was scheduled to be in Wolf Creek for weeks, maybe longer, he'd have plenty of time to learn more about the McClouds.

And the lovely Abigail Foster.

Chapter Three

Two days after Quinn arrived in Wolf Creek, the town's Chamber of Commerce hosted an informal, after-work gathering to introduce the business owners and town residents to their new temporary sheriff.

The party was held in the banquet room of the restaurant owned by Raine McCloud and her brother Trey Harper.

Chase McCloud hailed Quinn when he entered the room.

"Hey, Quinn." He beckoned, waiting to continue until Quinn joined them. "I'd like you to meet my wife, Raine."

Quinn shook the pretty brunette's slim hand, appreciating her firm grip and the smile in her gray eyes.

"Chase says we're very lucky to have you in Wolf Creek, Quinn." She glanced up at her husband, her eyes twinkling before her gaze met Quinn's once more. "I'm looking forward to hearing your version of stories about working at Colter Investigations with Chase. I'm guessing there are lots of things he's never told me."

Chase cocked an eyebrow, a smile tugging at the line of his mouth. "And he's not going to tell you, either."

The love and affection between the two was palpable. Chase draped his arm over Raine's shoulder and tucked her closer. The swell of her belly beneath the loose green maternity dress reminded Quinn why he was filling in as sheriff instead of Chase. Raine's pregnancy had had a few difficulties and the baby was due in a couple of months—around Thanksgiving, Quinn thought he remembered being told, probably by Ren. Chase had flatly refused to commit to a job whose responsibilities meant he could be on call around the clock. The fearless bounty hunter apparently had an Achilles' heel and her name was Raine. He wouldn't leave his wife alone under any circumstances.

Chase glanced past Quinn's shoulder and smiled. "Here's my sister and her husband. And my brother Luke and his wife."

Quinn was introduced to Zach Kerrigan and his wife, Jessie, Chase's sister, and their brother Luke McCloud and his wife, Rachel. The seven only had time to exchange a few moments of conversation before he was drawn away by the town mayor, Jim Pettigrew, and introduced to Walt Connors, owner of the auction barn where the annual horse sale took place.

"Good to meet you, Quinn." Walt's handshake was firm, his hand rough with calluses. "Sure is a coincidence—your last name bein' McCloud. We've had McClouds here in Wolf Creek for probably a hundred years. John McCloud and his boys run the biggest spread in the county."

"So I understand," Quinn said with a nod. "In fact, Chase McCloud is the reason I'm here. He and his partner own the investigative agency in Seattle where I work."

"Is that right?" The older man's shrewd gaze met Quinn's. "You sure you're not related to John and his boys, somehow?"

"I'm from New Mexico," Quinn replied with a grin, managing not to lie by not actually responding to the question. None of the McClouds knew he was a cousin and he had no plans to disclose the connection. "Never been to Montana before."

"Huh." Walt stared hard at Quinn for another moment before he shrugged. "Well, I don't mind tellin' you I'm glad you're here. I've been worried about security for the November horse auction. Not that we've had a lot of trouble in the past," he added. "But the last event held at the barn was a cattle sale and a bunch of folks from out of state brought in alcohol and got rowdy. Just last week, I talked to a friend at an auction barn in Colorado and he's hiring extra security for his next big sale. Sheriff Adams always had a plan long before folks started arriving in town. We talked about maybe adding some private security this year, but he didn't have time to get that done before he passed away."

"I heard his death was sudden," Quinn replied.

"Yeah." Walt's gray brows lowered in a frown, his lined face doleful. "A heart attack—he was in his kitchen. Doc said he was gone before he hit the floor." He shook his head. "It was a helluva shock for all of us. He was only sixty-eight, practically a kid."

Quinn's eyes widened a fraction. He wondered how old that made Walt, but he didn't ask. Instead, he only nodded.

"Be that as it may, Walt," the mayor interjected, "the November sale at your barn will go on as planned. And we're lucky you could fill in here until we can hire a permanent sheriff, Quinn."

"As it turns out, the timing was good for me, too," Quinn said. "I was between jobs and a temporary assignment here in Montana is more to my liking than hanging out in Seattle. I'm not partial to weeks of rain."

"Can't say as I blame you," Walt said. "I've seen it forty below zero here in January with snowbanks eight feet high. But I'll take snow before rain any day. Wet days make my bones ache."

"So does cold weather, Walt," the mayor said, grinning when the older man harrumphed in response.

Jim Pettigrew had told Quinn earlier, when he'd stopped in at the sheriff's office to introduce himself, that he'd known Walt for forty years. Quinn could see for himself that the two had an easy friendship and wondered briefly what it would be like to spend nearly half a century getting to know someone. He couldn't get his mind around the concept. The longest he'd ever remained anywhere was the ten years he'd spent in the army, but even then, he'd rarely been stationed on a base longer than a year.

"The Foster girls are here," Walt said abruptly. He pointed a gnarled finger over Quinn's left shoulder.

Quinn glanced behind him, his gaze zeroing in on Abby and her great-aunts. They managed to progress only a few feet into the room before they were greeted by three women and two men of varying ages.

"Good-looking women, those Fosters," Walt declared.

There was an undercurrent of pride in his deep voice. Intrigued, Quinn turned back to find Walt eyeing him.

When a moment passed, it became clear that Walt expected him to comment.

"I'd have to agree," he said with a grin.

Walt nodded, a jerk of his chin that told Quinn he approved. "Abigail looks a lot like Elizabeth," Walt said. "Acts like her, too, and runs that library like a general, I've heard say." His eyes narrowed over Quinn. "She's got grit. I always liked a woman with grit, how about you, son?"

"Uh, yeah, I'd have to say we agree on that, too." Quinn wondered where Walt was going with this. A moment later, he found out.

"Heard you're renting the apartment over the Fosters' garage, that right?" Walt asked.

"Yes." Quinn now had no doubts. Walt was sounding more and more like a father, trying to determine Quinn's intentions toward a daughter.

Walt grunted, continuing to eye Quinn critically. "I reckon it's a good thing they'll have a man on the premises, for protection, in case the auction crowds get rowdy this year."

"There won't be rowdy crowds in town for the auction, Walt," Jim protested. "The security will be in place and out-of-towners will be just as well behaved as they usually were when Chuck was alive. Right, Quinn?"

"Absolutely," Quinn said gravely. "Everybody in town will be as safe as good security protection can make them. You have my word on it." He spoke directly to Walt, looking him squarely in the eye.

Walt nodded abruptly. "Glad to hear it. Well, then…I think I'll go say hello to Elizabeth." He shook Quinn's hand and was gone, making his way through the clumps of people crowding the room.

"Is he related to the Foster women, by any chance?" Quinn asked, watching as Abby turned, her face lighting with pleasure as she smiled up at Walt and hugged him with enthusiasm.

"A cousin on Elizabeth and Natasha's mother's side," Jim replied. "He's always been protective of them, more like a brother than a cousin. And he's partial to Abigail— and her to him, too."

Quinn sipped his drink, thoughtfully studying Abby's animated features. "Any other relatives I should know about?"

"Probably, although I don't see any in the room right now." The mayor laughed. "One thing you can be sure of in Wolf Creek—nearly everyone you meet is likely to be related to someone else in town."

Quinn shook his head. "Not much like Seattle."

"No, I suppose not."

A middle-aged man and his wife interrupted them and the mayor introduced them as the owners of the minimart on the outskirts of Wolf Creek. The two were the first of a steady stream of local business owners who wanted to meet the new sheriff. Though he shook hands and carried on conversations, Quinn was always aware of Abigail's whereabouts.

He couldn't help but notice that she was treated with the same deference as her elderly aunts. Baffled and intrigued, he couldn't come up with a logical explanation as to why men weren't hitting on her right and left. The only plausible reason seemed to be that the men in Wolf Creek were all wearing invisible blinders.

* * *

Abigail was aware of Quinn the moment she and her aunts entered the banquet room. He was across the room, his back to her as he talked with the mayor and her great-aunts' cousin, eighty-year-old Walt Connors.

She saw Walt say something as he pointed at the doorway and Quinn glanced over his shoulder. Her gaze met his for one brief, electric moment before several friends and neighbors surrounded her and her great-aunts, claiming her attention.

As she circulated and said hello to the other guests, she took advantage of the opportunity to watch Quinn's easy charm as he interacted with the townsfolk. Women smiled at him, men grinned and pumped his hand. Abigail couldn't help but wonder if she was the only one aware of the core of steel beneath his undeniable charm.

As she extricated herself from the clutches of Sheila Hansen, town gossip, Abigail's gaze flickered over the gathering, unconsciously searching for Quinn.

He was half a room away, standing with Chase McCloud and Zach Kerrigan. She was struck by the resemblance between the three. Her eyes narrowed consideringly. All three men had coal-black hair and were easily over six feet tall, their bodies powerfully built. She knew Quinn and Chase were both connected to Colter Investigations and that Zach had been in the military before returning to run the family ranch in Wolf Creek. Was it their years spent in dangerous occupations that gave them an aura of easy command? And was it their subtle air of danger and power that made her think they looked alike—especially Quinn and Chase?

Probably, she told herself, turning her back on the compelling trio. *In any event, it's nothing to do with me beyond an interesting bit of trivia.*

Determined to stop focusing on Quinn, she refused to let herself keep tabs on him. She managed to avoid searching the crowd for him over the next hour, until her stomach rumbled with hunger, reminding her it had been a long time since lunch. Leaving her aunts chatting with Reverend Johnson about floral arrangements for the upcoming Sunday service, she made her way to the buffet table and collected a plate. It was clear most of the guests had already eaten. The selection wasn't encouraging, but Abigail chose an assortment of small, bite-size cheese slices and a handful of crackers. Celery and carrot sticks, accompanied by a spoonful of creamy Roquefort dip, were her next choices before she added a slice of fresh pineapple and three plump, perfect strawberries.

"Come have dinner with me. I'll buy you a steak to go with that."

Quinn's deep voice sounded much too close to her ear, his breath ghosting over her cheek.

Abigail shivered, muscles clenching low in her abdomen. Carefully, she turned her head and her gaze met his. His gray eyes were pewter-dark and warm. The faint scent of male cologne reached her as he leaned closer, seeming to loom larger, blocking out the rest of the room and its crowd of people. Heat washed over her, her fingers gripping the china plate harder in a vain attempt to stop her control from dissolving.

She struggled to form a reply. Her senses urged her to lean forward, bury her face against his throat and breathe in that elusive male scent that seemed to be his alone.

"It would be rude to leave the party so early," she got out.

He shrugged, his gaze refusing to release hers. "I've been here an hour and a half, talked to everyone in the room and it's way past dinnertime. I don't think anyone would object. In fact," he added, "quite a few people have already left."

He glanced behind him and her gaze followed his. He was right, she realized. The room that had been crowded when she and her great-aunts arrived was now only half-full, with more folks calling good-night and heading for the exit as she watched.

"Come with me, Abby." His deep drawl was mesmerizing. "You know you want to."

Abby stared, fascinated by the darkening of his gray eyes and the awareness that felt as if a web spun between them, heating the air separating them and pulling her closer.

Oh, no, she thought with sudden clarity. *I am in such trouble with you, Quinn.*

"I'm sorry," she managed to tell him without a flicker

of conscience that she lied. "But I have a ton of work I have to finish tonight and need to head home."

She knew he didn't believe her, but before he could say anything, she spun on her heel and headed for the door.

Sometimes, retreat was the better part of valor. And in this instance, Abigail though it was definitely the smartest plan.

Chapter Four

Two mornings later, Abigail grabbed her leather backpack and left the house by the back door, crossing the lawn to the garage. The spot usually occupied by Quinn's silver pickup was empty, and she wondered briefly why she hadn't heard him leave earlier.

She ignored a quick flash of disappointment and walked briskly to the wheeled trash can that was stored beneath the staircase. The rubber carrier was fully loaded and heavy. She leaned her weight into it and pushed, managing to roll it out from beneath the stairs and swing it toward the alley. The apartment door opened above her and she halted to look up.

Buddy bounded down the stairs, barking in greeting. Above him, the door closed and Quinn's boots sounded on the treads as he descended.

"Good morning, Abigail." He strolled toward her. His brown leather jacket hung open over a blue button-down shirt tucked into belted jeans. His black hair gleamed as if he'd just left the shower and his eyes were heavy lidded, sleepy. "Let me get that."

"Thanks." Abigail tore her fascinated gaze away from the clean-shaven line of his jaw and the curve of his mouth and willingly relinquished her grip on the handle of the heavy trashcan. She pointed at the alleyway where another dark green rubber container sat. "It goes over there, next to that one."

"What have you got in here, rocks?" Quinn asked as he easily wheeled the can to the alley and jockeyed it into place.

"Of course not," Abigail replied, amused. "Natasha cleaned and organized the garage. I have no idea what she threw away but I'm fairly sure it's not rocks."

"Maybe she tossed a car engine in there," Quinn commented dusting his hands off.

"Let's hope not," Abigail said dryly. She glanced at the empty parking spot. "What happened to your truck?"

"It's parked behind the office. I rode with Karl on a late call last night. He dropped me off here."

"And you're going in to work late this morning because you worked late last night?"

"Yeah. I can manage to function on four hours of sleep but three hours just makes me cranky." He tucked his hands in his jeans pockets, the corner of his mouth lifting in a half grin. "Mind if I walk you to work this morning, Miss Abigail?"

His teasing drawl sent a shiver of excitement and pure pleasure through Abigail's midsection. She pushed it down and told herself to stop reacting to him like a teenager with her first crush. "Of course I don't mind." She glanced at Buddy. "Is he going to the office, too?"

"Oh, yeah." Quinn whistled, and Buddy left his investigation of the grass near the neighbor's back fence and loped toward them. "He's become sort of a mascot. The dispatcher loves him."

"I'm not surprised," Abigail commented as the big dog nudged her hand with his nose. She smoothed her hand over his silky ears, smiling when his brown eyes half closed with pleasure. "He's a sweetie."

The three walked down the alley and turned right, passing the front of the Foster house.

The morning air was brisk and Abigail buttoned her scarlet jacket to her chin. She glanced sideways. Quinn's hands were tucked in his jacket pockets but he hadn't zipped it closed. "Aren't you chilly?"

"No, why?" His gaze skimmed her from head to toe before returning, the perusal growing heated. "I'm warm."

She knew her cheeks were turning pink but she

refused to drop her gaze from his. "You have to stop flirting with me."

His lips tilted at the corners. "Why? What fun would that be?"

She ignored the question. "You're wasting your time. If you're looking for fun, you need to look elsewhere." She was pleased with the level of firmness she managed to inject into her voice. Especially when her body was objecting so strongly and urging her to find out what he meant by "fun."

The sound of a rich, deeply amused chuckle snapped her gaze back to his face. His eyes sparkled with mirth.

"Does that usually work with guys?" he asked.

"I have no idea what you're talking about," she lied, tilting her chin. Since leaving college and returning to Wolf Creek, she'd found a few blunt, sharp comments had always sent men running. She'd never wanted to purposely hurt anyone's feelings, but she was convinced that ultimately it was less harmful if she made it clear early on that she wasn't interested in a relationship.

"Really?" he said mildly, though his eyes laughed at her.

She looked away, unwilling to hold his gaze as her cheeks grew warmer. Somehow, she was reluctant to have this conversation, despite knowing this was an opportunity to convince Quinn he should turn his attention elsewhere.

Before she could decide what to say, Quinn abruptly changed the subject.

"Did you grow up in the neighborhood?

"Yes, I did. Why?"

He pointed at the neat square of the park edged by the sidewalk. "I wondered if you played here."

Abigail realized she'd been so distracted by Quinn that she hadn't noticed they'd reached the playground. The limbs of the old maple trees were lit with red and gold color, while piles of fallen leaves lay in drifts around the base of their thick trunks. Leaves were also scattered over the neatly mowed expanses of green lawn and on the sand beneath the children's slide and swings.

She couldn't help but smile. "I love this park—I played here nearly every day when I was little."

"So your parents lived near your aunts?"

"I actually grew up at my aunts' house. My dad and I went to live with them after my mother passed away."

"I'm sorry to hear that." His voice was quiet, somber. "It must have been tough, losing your mother."

Abigail glanced at him and her steps slowed. His face was grave, his gray eyes dark with what she thought was sympathy as his gaze met hers.

"I was very young," she said softly, not realizing that they'd stopped to face each other. "Too young to remember her."

"That doesn't make it okay. Sometimes, it makes it worse."

"Yes, exactly." She searched his face. "Very few people understand that."

"My father died before I was born." He shrugged. "Doesn't make it any easier that you never had a chance to know them. They're still gone. And you have no memories to fall back on."

She had the sudden urge to reach out, wrap her arms around him and hold him close. Whether she wanted to seek comfort or give it, she didn't know. Before she could act on the impulse, however, Buddy bounded toward them across the grass of the park, his barks demanding their attention and shattering the emotionally charged moment.

Quinn bent and took the stick from the dog's mouth. Buddy instantly sat, his tail swishing across the sidewalk's concrete, eyes lit with anticipation.

Then Quinn tossed the stick, sending it sailing over the stretch of grass, and Buddy raced after it, barking.

Both adults laughed as they watched him streak away. The dog slid to a halt, grabbed the stick in his teeth and spun to race back to them.

"This could go on for hours," Quinn said dryly. "Sorry, Buddy, no more playing." He rubbed his palm over the dog's blond head and grinned at Abigail. "If you're going to get to work on time, we'll have to play fetch with Buddy later."

They chatted casually as they walked the remaining blocks downtown. Quinn and Buddy left Abigail at the bottom of the library steps, angling across the street to disappear into the sheriff's office.

As she unlocked doors and went inside, Abigail realized that the morning's walk had changed something between them. The common experience of losing a parent while very young had created a bond, a level of comfort between them that had slipped past her defenses and caught her unaware.

Despite her determination to distance herself from Quinn, she thought, she was finding she liked him.

Quinn McCloud was nothing like the men she'd dealt with over the past few years. How was she to hold him at arm's length when he simply laughed at her sharp comments, looked at her with sympathetic understanding—and refused to go away?

That evening Abigail walked briskly down the sidewalk, her backpack slung over her shoulder. The crisp late-afternoon air held the smell of wood smoke. Fallen leaves crunched beneath her feet as she passed under the maples lining her street.

Elizabeth and Natasha had left earlier in the morning on a shopping expedition with a friend. They planned to stay overnight in Billings and return home the following morning, which meant Abigail would have the house to herself. Much as she enjoyed her aunts' company, a little alone time wasn't a bad thing.

She was looking forward to kicking off her shoes, pouring a glass of wine, and heating the lasagna left from the night before. She quickened her steps as she neared her front yard.

Unlatching the gate, she pushed it wide, pausing to look over her shoulder when a car turned the corner at the end of the block. The rumble of an aging muffler grew more pronounced as the vehicle accelerated down the street toward her, then slowed as it drew new near. The car suddenly braked to swerve close to the curb behind her, stopping abruptly. Abigail didn't recognize either the vehicle nor the people inside and wondered if they needed directions.

The passenger door thrust open, releasing a burst of loud rock music underlaid with the heavy pound of drums, and a teenage girl climbed out.

"Hi," she called with an engaging grin. "Do you live here? Do you know Elizabeth Foster?"

"Elizabeth is my aunt," Abigail replied as she turned to face the car, wondering who the girl was and what her connection could be to Elizabeth.

"Cool." The girl tugged the passenger seat forward and leaned into the back seat. "Come on, kid. This is the place."

The teenager tugged a little girl forward and out onto the sidewalk. The child eyed Abigail with misgiving, tucking her chin against her chest and lowering her lashes. The older girl leaned into the back seat once again and pulled out a large duffel bag and a blanket.

"Here we go." She caught the little girl by the hand and hurried her across the sidewalk to Abigail. "This is Tansy. She's staying with Elizabeth until her daddy gets home."

Abigail blinked in surprise. "She is?"

"Yeah." The teenager smacked her forehead with the palm of her hand. "Oh, crap, I forgot. The letter."

She dropped the duffel and darted back to the car, faded jeans pulling tightly over her slender backside when she leaned into the front seat.

Despite the noisy music, Abigail caught fragments of conversation between the teenaged male driver and the girl, and knew she was searching for something.

"Here it is." The girl darted back to Abigail, waving a square envelope. "Tansy's grandmother wrote a note that explains everything."

Abigail took the envelope from her outstretched hand. It was damp.

"Oh, yeah. I spilled some soda on it. Sorry about that," she said airily.

"Come on, Nikki, we're going to be late," the driver yelled over the music.

The girl glanced at the car. "All right, all right! I'm coming." She turned back and grinned apologetically at Abigail. "Gotta go. We have concert tickets and it's a long drive home." She bent and drew the little girl into a quick hug. "Be good, kiddo. I'll see you soon."

Stunned, Abigail realized the teenager was leaving. "Wait," she said. "You can't just leave without explaining...."

"Sorry—have to—we're late," the girl said as she ran to the car and jumped in. "Read the note," she called as she was closing the door.

The girl was barely inside before the car accelerated away from the curb in a rush of engine noise and noxious exhaust fumes.

Abigail considered running after the vehicle and attempting to stop them so she could demand a better explanation, but they were gone before she could rally her thoughts. She looked at the little girl. The child's thick-lashed, big blue eyes were wary and she gripped her blanket tight.

Abigail smiled reassuringly. "Well, I think we should go read your grandmother's note. Is that okay with you?"

The child nodded slowly.

Abigail stepped closer and held out her hand. "I suggest you come inside with me. We'll read the note from your grandmother and have some dinner. I'll telephone Elizabeth and get this straightened out. She's on a trip to Billings and won't be home until tomorrow, but I know where she's staying."

Big blue eyes studied her for a long moment, doubtful, before she put her little hand in Abigail's.

"Promise?" she asked, searching Abigail's face.

"I promise," Abigail said solemnly, and sketched an *X* over her left breast. "Cross my heart."

"Okay."

Abigail was well aware how hesitant the little girl was—the small body fairly vibrated with uncertainty. Nevertheless, she walked beside Abigail up the walk and onto the porch.

Abigail unlocked and pushed the door wide, then stepped over the threshold, allowing Tansy to follow while she flipped the light switch on the wall next to the door. Lamps in the entry and parlor sprang to life, their warm glow instantly making the big old-fashioned rooms cozy and welcoming. She ushered the little girl down the hall to the kitchen.

"I don't know about you, but I'm starved. You can put your things down on a chair over there." She pointed at the big corner nook. The little girl obeyed, the chair legs scraping against the tiled floor when she pulled it out. The blanket draped over the bag on the wooden seat, half concealing it as the brown wool trailed onto the floor. Tansy carefully arranged the tattered teddy bear on top.

"Let's see what your grandmother said in her note," Abigail said when Tansy pulled out a second chair, climbed onto the seat and looked at her expectantly.

The envelope was very damp on one end. Abigail carefully tore it open and slid out a single sheet. The paper was dry on the left half but distinctly wet on the right where the ink had smudged and blurred the words. Some were barely legible.

Dear Elizabeth, My neighbor is writing this note for me because the paramedics tell me I've had a heart attack and must go to the hospital immediately. I am the sole caretaker of my granddaughter, Tansy, and am sending her to you, my dear friend, trusting that you will

care for her until I'm released from hospital or until my
son-in-law arrives home and can come get her. I know
we haven't talked in such a long time but I have no one
else to turn to. I know I can rely upon our unfailing good
heart and our friendship in this emergency.

Abigail frowned, trying to decipher the signature. The note was written in a firm hand, the letters almost block-like. But the signature had clearly been penned with shaking fingers, the letters nearly illegible. The damp paper had also made the ink smear, which only made it more difficult to read.

"I can't quite read the signature," Abigail said to the little girl. "Can you tell me your grandmother's name?"

"Grandma Jane," the child said promptly.

"And do you know her last name?" When the little girl shook her head, Abigail tried a new tack. "What about your name?"

"My name is Tansy Smith and I'm four years old." She said promptly, holding up four little fingers.

"I see," Abigail smiled encouragingly. "And your mommy and daddy's names?"

"I don't have a mommy 'cause she went to heaven. My daddy's name is Joseph and he's in 'ganistan."

"I'm sorry to hear about your mother," Abigail said gently. "Is your daddy in the military in Afghanistan?"

Long hair bounced as she nodded vigorously. "He's a soldier. Grandma said he'll come get me soon."

"I'm sure he will," Abigail said with a firm, reassuring nod. Privately, she hoped Elizabeth knew who "Grandma Jane" was, because if not, how in the world would they contact her or Tansy's father? Abigail held little hope that the two teenagers who'd dropped Tansy off would check back with her. Which meant Elizabeth was the best hope to solve the mystery that was Tansy.

"Now, then," Abigail said briskly as she picked up the phone. "I'm going to call Aunt Elizabeth and let her know you're here, okay?"

"'Kay." Tansy nodded.

Abigail tapped in Elizabeth's cell phone number but was sent to voice mail. She left a quick message and rang off, then dialed the home number of her aunts' friend in Billings where the two were spending the night. The answering machine picked up and she left a message, asking Elizabeth to call home, then rang off and returned the portable phone to its base.

"They're not answering," she told Tansy, who watched her with solemn eyes. "But I'm sure Elizabeth will return my call as soon as she gets my message. In the meantime, I was planning to warm up lasagna and make a salad for dinner. How does that sound?"

"Yum." The little head nodded enthusiastically, her blue eyes lighting. "I love lasagna."

"Excellent. Why don't we go wash our hands and you can help me make a salad?"

"Okay."

After a quick trip to the bathroom where Abigail

took time to have Tansy wash not just her hands but her dusty face as well, Abigail tied a white chef's apron around the girl's waist, adjusting the white cotton to fit her small frame, and found a stool for her to stand on. Then she cut extra-large squares of lasagna and popped the first plate into the microwave.

She opened a cupboard door and took out a large bowl to mix the salad in, setting it on the counter in front of Tansy. "Your grandmother was very wise to send you to Elizabeth's house because all of us—my great-aunt Elizabeth, Natasha and me—love having visitors." She took the lid off the spinner. "Now, let's make the salad. I'm really hungry, aren't you?"

Tansy nodded and set to with a will.

Abigail hoped the little girl was reassured about her welcome in the Foster home. Her apprehension appeared to have disappeared as they set the table and sat down to eat. The amount of food the little girl put away was staggering.

The growl of an engine interrupted Abigail's thoughts and headlights swept an arc over the kitchen windows. Quinn was home.

Of course, she thought with relief. She'd ask Quinn to help.

"That's my neighbor's truck," she told Tansy as she pushed back her chair and stood. "I'll be right back."

Tansy nodded, her mouth too full of lasagna to reply.

By the time Abigail opened the back door, Quinn was

at the base of the stairs at the garage, his hand on the rail, and Buddy was nosing about under the maple tree.

"Quinn?"

He turned at her call, strolling toward her when she beckoned. "What's up?"

"Two teenagers dropped off a little girl just as I came home from work." Quickly she told him the strange story. "Hopefully Elizabeth will call back soon, but in the meantime, would you talk to her? Perhaps you can learn something—some clue that would tell us who her family is and where she came from."

"She can't tell you her parents' names?"

"No. And I don't want to pressure her because she's obviously exhausted and scared."

"I'll come in and talk to her."

"Don't act like a cop," Abigail said quickly. "I don't want her to feel threatened."

Quinn stopped and looked down at her, gray eyes narrowing. "You think I'd purposely scare a kid?"

"No, of course not. Well, maybe." She shrugged and lifted her hands. "How should I know what you'd do? I've never seen you in action. I've only seen cops on TV—and they scare adults, let alone a little girl in a strange house with strange people."

He muttered an oath and lifted his gaze skyward. Abigail thought she heard him counting to ten, then he straightened. "I'm not an idiot."

"I didn't say you were," Abigail protested. But she

was talking to his back as he strode ahead of her into the house. A cold, damp nose bumped her hand and she jumped, looking down. "Hey, Buddy. Want to come in?"

The Lab panted, pink tongue lolling as he grinned at her and brushed past to lope happily ahead into the house.

"Males." Abigail closed the door with a snap behind her and followed them.

"Hey, how's it goin'?"

She heard Quinn's deep-toned, casual comment followed by Tansy's murmured "fine". When she entered the kitchen, Quinn was taking a plate from the open cupboard.

She lifted an eyebrow when he turned and found her watching him.

"Looks like you two started dinner without me, Abigail." He cut a chunk of lasagna, ladled it onto the plate and slid the plate into the microwave. Then he shrugged out of his jacket and walked to the breakfast nook. He hung the coat over the back of the chair facing Tansy. "I'm Quinn," he said easily. "Who are you?"

"Tansy Smith." She eyed him from beneath her lashes, chin dipped until it nearly tucked against her chest.

"This is Buddy," Quinn told Tansy, rubbing one hand over the Lab's head and silky ears.

Tansy stared at the big yellow dog, clearly fascinated, but she didn't comment.

Abigail noted the little fingers, wrapped tightly around the fork, and shot Quinn a worried glance.

He merely smiled at her, patting her shoulder with easy familiarity when he walked by her on his way to the cupboard. Abigail was still trying to get her breathing back to normal when she heard water running in the sink behind her and the splash as he washed his hands. A drawer opened, closed and then he strolled past again, on his way back to the table with a bowl for salad and cutlery.

The microwave pinged and Abigail snapped to life. "I'll get it."

"Thanks." Quinn shot her a friendly smile.

She knew he was purposely creating a friendly, cozy impression to make Tansy comfortable, but somehow she was getting sucked in to believing it, too. *Get a grip,* she told herself, *he's just doing his job—and he's amazingly good at it. He should have become an actor, maybe an action-adventure movie star instead of a real-life warrior.*

She carried the hot plate of lasagna to the table and set it in front of him, then took her own seat.

"How was work?" Quinn asked.

Following his lead, Abigail chatted casually about her day. Both adults kept the conversation low-key, each unobtrusively monitoring Tansy's level of comfort. The little fingers gradually loosened on the fork and she began to eat again.

"This is great lasagna—did you help make it, Tansy?" Quinn's casual question came out of the blue.

"No. But I washed the lettuce for the salad," she replied.

"Excellent salad." Quinn nodded solemnly. "Good job."

She smiled shyly and drank her milk, eyeing him over the rim of the glass.

"Especially for a three-year-old," Quinn continued.

"I'm not three." Tansy frowned at him.

"No?" Quinn lifted his eyebrows in disbelief. "Are you sure?"

"Of course I'm sure. I'm four," she said proudly, squaring her shoulders and lifting her chin. "And I'm a big girl. I know my numbers and I can write my name and everything."

"My apologies for thinking you were three because you're obviously much older. And Tansy is a pretty name," Quinn said. "I don't think I've ever known a girl named Tansy. I bet that was your mama's name, too, right?"

"No." She shook her head.

"Then I'm guessing her name was…." Quinn winked at her and grinned. "Hortensia."

A snort of laughter surprised Tansy and she nearly choked on her milk. "That's not a name!"

"Yup. It is," Quinn insisted. "I bet that was your mom's name—Hortensia Smith."

"Noooooooo." She shook her head. "It's not Hortensia."

"Then it's Tansy Smith, just like yours."

"Nope." She eyed him, eyes shining with mischief.

"Let's see, how about Georgia? Henrietta?" Quinn named a long list of silly names and had Tansy giggling. "How about Nikki?"

She shook her head.

"Nikki's a nice name." Quinn looked at Abigail. "Maybe not as nice as Elizabeth. Or Abigail," he said mildly.

Abigail didn't look at Tansy, but she was very aware of the child. "I always envied my aunt Elizabeth and wished I'd been named after her." She kept her response in the same light tone Quinn had used.

"Who were you named after?" Quinn's voice held mild curiosity as he calmly emptied his plate and stood to carry it to the sink.

"My mother." She glanced at Tansy. "I was raised by my two great-aunts, Elizabeth and Natasha, after my own mother died when I was a baby and my dad needed help. That's why I know what a nice house this is for a little girl." She smiled confidingly and stood, gathering up her own plate and utensils and joining Quinn at the sink.

Her look asked him if they'd interviewed the tired little girl enough for the night. His barely perceptible nod told her yes. She sighed with relief and turned back to the table.

"I don't know about you two, but I'm ready to change into my jammies and get comfortable." Beside her, Quinn's body tensed. *Oh, great,* she thought, pushing away an instant mental image of Quinn joining her in…whatever he wore to bed, nothing, maybe? She slammed the door on her imagination and walked back to the table and Tansy.

"Would you like to come upstairs with me? We'll find you some pajamas and a toothbrush."

"I have jammies in my bag—and my toothbrush, too. But I don't have toothpaste."

"That's okay, you can use mine."

Tansy pushed back her empty plate and hopped down. "I'll get my bag."

Abigail met Quinn's gaze. "Tansy's staying in my old room upstairs." It wasn't a question.

He shrugged. "You ladies do your thing—I'm heading over to my place with Buddy. We'll see you in the morning."

"'Bye, Mr. Quinn."

"Good night, Tansy." He snapped his fingers and Buddy rose from the braided rug in front of the sink. "I'll see you tomorrow, Abigail."

"Good night, Quinn."

"Thanks for dinner."

"You're welcome." Abigail's eyes narrowed as she looked at him.

He grinned unrepentantly and left the kitchen.

"I'm ready."

Abigail realized she was staring at the door panels, wondering why she felt as if there was more going on here than his assisting with Tansy. The little girl's voice snapped her out of her reverie.

"Great, let's go upstairs."

A half hour later, Tansy was washed, scrubbed,

dressed in Dora the Explorer knit pajamas, with her damp hair brushed back off her brow. Abigail had changed into her own pajamas while Tansy splashed and played in the big tub.

Tansy's eyelids were drooping when she climbed into bed. Abigail tucked the covers under her chin, leaving only the small face visible with the bedraggled teddy bear next to it.

"Good night, Tansy. Sleep tight."

"'Night," she murmured, lashes already drifting lower.

Abigail tiptoed out of the room but left the door open. If the child woke in the night and was frightened in a strange house, she wanted to be sure she could hear her.

She returned to the kitchen and found herself staring out the window as she rinsed the dinner dishes, her gaze drawn inexorably across the back lawn to the apartment above the garage.

The drapes were closed over the living room window, but it glowed with light from within.

Abigail wondered what Quinn was doing. Watching TV? Reading? What did he do in his free time? She didn't know him well enough to make a guess. And she probably never would.

When the town council hired a permanent sheriff, Quinn would leave, moving on to the next Colter Investigations assignment. She shouldn't let herself be so attracted to him. There was no future in it and in truth, a great deal of danger. Not physical, of course, but emotional? Definitely.

Just like her dead husband.

Only Elizabeth and Natasha knew about her short, six-month marriage. She and Manny met in a senior math class at UCLA and she'd fallen head over heels in love with him. They eloped to Las Vegas three months later, were married in an all-night chapel and set up housekeeping in student housing on campus.

But she'd soon learned the charming, devil-may-care young man she'd adored and married had a thrill seeker bent and a thirst for danger that was unquenchable. When he died six months later in a car accident—he'd been racing with a friend—the tangled heap of metal wasn't even recognizable as having once been a car. She was devastated and inconsolable with grief. She'd barely managed to complete school, returning home to the quiet of Wolf Creek to grieve and allow her broken heart to mend.

She'd vowed never again to risk her heart. Especially with a man addicted to danger. She'd learned a valuable lesson about the pain of loving the wrong man.

And while she knew that Quinn's current occupation as a police officer wasn't the same as Manny's obsession with risking his life for the rush, she couldn't get past the details on Quinn's résumé. He'd worked in so many dangerous countries around the world that Abigail couldn't remember all the names.

No, a career spent in the military and law enforcement certainly wasn't on par with a young man seeking never-ending thrills. But for Abigail, the underlying drive was the same—a willingness to risk their lives on a daily basis. And god save anyone who cared about them if they lost the game.

Collateral damage, she thought. *That's what I was when Manny slammed into that concrete wall at a hundred and twenty miles an hour. And that's what I'll be if I give in to my curiosity about Quinn.*

She wished she were more like her girlfriends. They seemed able to fall in love, have a good time, then move on without suffering for longer than a few days, or weeks.

She, on the other hand, had spent years recovering from Manny's death.

Face it, Abigail, she told herself. *You're terrified to care about Quinn because you're afraid he could break your heart.*

She shook her head at her own timidity.

But it wasn't about being afraid, she argued with herself. What kind of a fool would she be if she walked, with open eyes, into a relationship that she knew could only end badly?

But think about the days you'd have with him, a small voice inside her whispered temptingly, the roller-coaster thrill of making love, shared hours. The thought of getting naked with Quinn made her heart race.

She yanked open the dishwasher door and loaded the plates into the racks.

If she didn't stop thinking about getting naked with Quinn she was going to have a meltdown.

Disappointed at her inability to solve the puzzle that was Tansy, Abigail tried telephoning Elizabeth once more but had to go to bed without reaching her.

Sunshine poured into the big kitchen the following morning. Tansy sat at the breakfast corner nook, eating a bowl of cereal. Abigail was at the counter, putting together sandwiches for their lunch, when someone knocked on the back door.

Abigail glanced out the window. Quinn stood on her back step, Buddy cruising nose to the ground a few yards away.

She glanced at Tansy as she walked across the kitchen to the door. The little girl had stopped eating, her eyes curious as she stared at the doorway.

"It's just Quinn and Buddy," Abigail reassured her. "Finish your cereal."

Abigail pulled open the door, tried to ignore the shiver of helpless attraction that shook her, and stood back to let Quinn enter the porch.

"Morning." His voice was rough, his eyes still sleepy.

"You don't appear to have been awake very long," she commented. "Late night?"

He yawned and rubbed his eyes. "I was called out after midnight. Fight at the tavern."

"I have coffee."

She turned and led the way into the kitchen. Buddy gave her a bump of his nose against her thigh in greeting as he brushed past her and headed for Tansy. Child and dog greeted each other with mutual delight.

Quinn leaned his hips against the counter next to Abigail and crossed his arms over his chest.

"Morning, Tansy," he drawled, his voice raspy.

"Good morning, Mr. Quinn," she replied before turning back to Buddy and her cereal.

"How did she do last night?" Quinn murmured to Abigail.

"She slept like a log." Abigail glanced over her shoulder. Tansy was laughing at Buddy, ignoring the adults. "I was afraid she'd wake in the night and being in a strange place would scare her, but she didn't stir until I went in to wake her around seven this morning."

"Good." He took the coffee mug she handed him, his fingers warm where they brushed hers. "Did you talk to Elizabeth last night?"

Abigail shook her head. "No. I'm sure she's forgotten to check her cell phone's voice mail."

"Are you taking Tansy to work with you today?"

"Yes, she can stay at the library with me until Elizabeth and Natasha are home."

"What time do you expect them?"

"Probably around eleven. They go on a shopping trip like this every month or so and typically, they're home before lunch."

He nodded. "Then I'll come by the library around eleven-thirty. We can beat the lunch rush at the café."

She hesitated before agreeing. "I'll call your office if Elizabeth hasn't arrived by eleven-fifteen. If I can't reach her by phone before we have to leave here at nine-thirty, I'll put a note on the table asking her to come to the library as soon as she gets home."

He lifted his mug in salute, then drained the coffee and handed her the mug. His gray eyes darkened for a moment and then he smiled, the flash of intimacy plain. "Thanks for the coffee, Abby." He looked across the room, snapping his fingers to call Buddy. "Bye, Tansy. Have a good day at the library."

"'Kay. Bye."

His departure seemed to take the oxygen from the room. Abigail leaned against the counter and drew in a deep breath. Why did one look from him make her heart race and her body yearn?

While Tansy got dressed, Abigail called Elizabeth's cell phone and again, had to leave a message. But her aunt's friend answered her phone on the second ring. Unfortunately, Elizabeth and Natasha had already left to drive back to Wolf Creek. The three women had gone to the theater the evening before and arrived home after midnight. Evidently none of them had thought to check for phone messages.

After writing a note asking Elizabeth to come to the library the moment she and Natasha arrived home, Abigail and Tansy left the house. It was only nine-thirty, but Tansy was so enthralled by the neighborhood park as they passed, the huge maple trees shading the streets, and the shops they walked by that it was nearly ten o'clock before they reached the library.

Across the street, Quinn stood at the front office counter, where he'd been for the last half hour. He'd glanced at his watch more than once since nine-forty and progressed from wondering where Abby and Tansy were to worrying that something had happened to them.

When he saw the two females, one adult, one much smaller, climb the steps to the library across the way, he was tempted to cross the street and ask Abby where she'd been.

But he curbed the impulse. He'd see her at lunch. He could wait. The fact that he still wanted to cross the street and talk to her was annoying as hell.

He purposely turned his back on the window with its view of the library and went into his office.

Chapter Five

The library's double doors opened wide, a gust of fresh fall air swooping inside. Abigail looked up from inspecting the binding of a worn copy of *Pride and Prejudice* to see Elizabeth and Natasha walking toward the counter. They nodded and smiled warmly at other patrons who said hello but didn't speak; their determination to obey the unwritten rule of maintaining quiet in the library made Abigail smile.

They reached the large oak station where Abigail stood and Elizabeth slipped Abigail's urgent message from that morning onto the smooth wooden countertop.

"Hello, dear." Elizabeth set a new blue leather Coach purse down next to the note.

Abigail raised an eyebrow. "Someone made a stop at the mall," she said in a low, admiring tone, smoothing her palm over the buttery soft texture of the bag.

Elizabeth's smile held satisfaction. "I told you it was a steal," she said to Natasha before turning back to Abigail. "Natasha thought I might be too old to carry such a cute bag."

"I said you might not need another cute bag," Natasha corrected. "because you have a closetful at home. You couldn't swing a cat in your room without hitting a cute bag, old or new," she teased.

"Ladies," Abigail murmured, pointing to the library's Quiet sign. "Take it outside."

Her aunts chuckled, the twinkle in each of their eyes pulling at Abigail's heart and making her so thankful for the two.

Elizabeth cleared her throat and tapped the note with her forefinger. "We're here, as requested. Now, just what is this mysterious note all about?"

A pair of chubby hands appeared at the edge of the station; then a tangle of brown hair over a childish forehead slowly became visible, then two enormous blue eyes that peered up at the two women.

Abigail patted Tansy on the head and gave her a reassuring smile before returning her gaze to her aunts. "Elizabeth, Natasha, I'd like you to meet Tansy." She closed her hands around the child's slender waist, picked her up and set her on the counter.

Both women beamed at the little girl, their love of children instantly obvious.

"I'm delighted to meet you, Tansy. My name is Elizabeth and this is my sister, Natasha."

"Oh!" the little girl chirped, turning her entire body to face Elizabeth. "My Grandma said I should stay with you until Daddy comes to get me and you would take care of me, like you took care of him!"

Elizabeth's questioning gaze met Abigail's.

"Tansy arrived last night with a note from her Grandma Jane, who apparently is an old friend of yours." Abigail slipped the note from her pocket and gave it to her great aunt.

Unfolding the slip of paper, Elizabeth quickly scanned it, then slowly read again. When she lifted her gaze to Abigail's, however, she seemed as confused as everyone else.

"I'm sorry, Abigail. Tansy's grandmother clearly knows me but the note isn't specific enough to jog my memory of her." She peered down at Tansy. "Do you know your Grandma Jane's full name, Tansy?"

But the little girl couldn't give them any information beyond her own name, insisting her small family was made up of herself, Daddy Joseph and Grandma Jane.

"Grandma Jane said you knew my daddy." Tansy's voice wobbled, her eyes filled with tears. "I didn't know I had to remember his soldier name. It's long."

Abigail ran a hand down the length of Tansy's thick

fall of hair. "It's all right, Tansy. You didn't do anything wrong."

"Of course not," Elizabeth added, shooting Abigail a slightly bewildered look before smiling gently at the little girl. "I don't know about you, but I would very much like a cookie break. Why don't you come home with Natasha and me and we'll see what we have in the cookie jar, shall we?"

A bright smile lit Tansy's face. Maybe now they would make some progress on finding out just where this little girl came from, Abigail thought with relief as she walked out from behind the counter.

"I'll see you at home tonight," she called after the three as they walked toward the door.

Tansy ran back at the last minute, gesturing for Abigail to lean down. She kissed her on the cheek. "See you later, alligator."

"After a while, crocodile," Abigail answered, then watched the little girl happily rejoin her aunts.

At exactly eleven twenty-five, Quinn strolled across the street and climbed the steps to the library.

The distinctive smell of paper, ink and binding glue from well-used books instantly reminded him of his school days. This was a Carnegie Library, built sometime around the turn of the century, maybe in the late 1800s or early 1900s, he guessed.

It had clearly been cherished during those hundred or so years, he thought, because it was in damn good shape.

The interior was trimmed in oak, with wainscoting lining the walls. Tall, solid-looking bookcases marched in stately rows along a central aisle. Brass lighting fixtures hung from the high ceiling, and a long oak library table with matching solid chairs sat in the space to the right of the door. The study area looked out through the windows at Wolf Creek's main street.

Ahead and to the left of Quinn was the librarian station. The horseshoe-shaped area was constructed of heavy dark oak, carved and elegant. Abigail stood on the other side, stamping the inside flyleaf of a stack of hardcover books while she chatted with an older woman.

Only a few short hours had passed since he'd left her kitchen but his body reacted as if it were starved for the sight of her. His heartbeat sped up, muscles tensed, and when she laughed at something the older woman said, the curve of Abigail's lush mouth was instantly arousing.

Damn, McCloud, get a grip.

Quinn strolled to the counter and Abigail looked up. "Good morning." He tucked his hands in his back pockets and nodded at the other woman.

The gray-haired woman returned his greeting, accepted her stack of books from Abigail and headed for the door.

"Ready to go?"

"Yes." She logged off the computer and walked to a desk in the corner of the area sectioned off by the counter. "Linda," she called as she opened a drawer and took out a black leather purse. "I'm leaving for lunch."

A woman in her mid-forties, flyaway brown hair piled on top of her head in a loose knot, appeared from one of the bookcase aisles toward the back of the room.

"Good morning, Sheriff." Her breezy greeting suggested they'd met, but for the life of him, Quinn couldn't place her. She grinned as she lifted the small section of hinged countertop to join Abigail. "I'm Linda Graves, we met at the get-together when you arrived in town. My husband owns the grocery store."

"Oh, right." Quinn nodded. "Sorry, I met a lot of people that night."

"Don't worry about it." She brushed off his apology with a quick grin, holding the section of counter up to allow Abigail to exit. "You'll learn all our names soon enough—we're a small community."

"I'll be back by twelve-thirty, Linda," Abigail said over her shoulder as she joined Quinn.

"Take your time—I don't have to meet Bill until one."

Quinn and Abigail left the library, his long strides easily keeping up with her brisk pace.

"What did Elizabeth tell you about Tansy?" he asked as they covered the short two blocks to the restaurant.

"She has no more idea who sent the child here than we do." Abigail glanced sideways, meeting his gaze. "I'd hoped she would unravel the mystery, but apparently she's as baffled as we are."

They reached the restaurant and further discussion was postponed while they were seated and the waitress took their order. When at last they were settled, Quinn sipped his coffee and eyed her. "What exactly did Tansy say when Elizabeth picked her up?"

"She told Elizabeth that her grandmother said she was to stay with Miss Elizabeth until he could come get her."

"And that's all?"

Abigail lifted her hands helplessly in a shrug. "That's the gist of it. We're all mystified by this."

Quinn rested his forearms on the table, turning the mug in slow circles between his palms on the wood. "I'll call Social Services when I get back to the office. They'll send someone out to pick up Tansy, probably this afternoon."

"No." Abigail's rejection was firm. "Absolutely not. She'll stay with us."

Quinn lifted an eyebrow. "She's an abandoned child, Abigail. I can't keep the information from the Department of Social and Health Services. There are specific rules governing procedures in a situation like this."

"I don't care. She seems comfortable with us and after the trauma of being left at a strange house, with unfamiliar people, it would be cruel to move her again." Abigail eyed him militantly, her jaw set.

"I'm not disagreeing," he said, trying to make her see reason. "But that doesn't mean I can break the law."

"Will you recommend Tansy be left in our care while you search for her family? At least for the short term?"

"I can do that. But it doesn't mean the social worker has to agree," he cautioned her. "The foster care system has rules."

"Will she have to go into a foster home?" Abigail's face paled.

"She'll be under the jurisdiction of the state system, I'm assuming. I'll have to make some calls and check the law."

"Why can't our home be her foster home?"

"Maybe it can. If you were related to her, it would be easier."

Her eyes narrowed and she leaned forward. "Why?"

"Because the rules are more lenient about approving family members to care for a child on a temporary basis. At least, they are in Washington. I'll have to check Montana law. And then you'll have to get the approval of the foster system."

"You can leave that to me," Abigail told him with assurance. "Between the three of us, my aunts and I know most everyone in the county. It's very likely Elizabeth or Natasha can have us assigned to be Tansy's foster home."

"Why do you care so much?" Quinn asked, curious. "You only met the kid yesterday."

Abigail stiffened. "I don't have to know her a long time to feel compassion for her situation. She's a child. And since she's settled at our house, she should stay there until her parents are found."

"I'm not disagreeing," Quinn said mildly. "I'm just asking."

"Hmph," Abigail sniffed, clearly only partially mollified by his concession. "I assume you'll notify us when you've talked to the social worker?"

"I can do that." He nodded, leaning back to let the waitress slide a plate with a cheeseburger and fries on the table in front of him.

They were silent for a moment while the waitress refilled coffee cups before she whisked away. Abigail tucked into her salad.

"I don't want to make Tansy feel I'm interrogating her," Quinn told her. "But she seems fairly comfortable having me around, and she likes Buddy."

"I'm relieved you don't want to question her directly," Abigail said with warmth. "She seems to stress out whenever anyone asks her direct questions about her father or grandmother."

"Makes sense. She's only four. Appears to be a fairly mature four-year-old, but still." He shrugged. "What are your plans for the weekend?"

She lifted an eyebrow in surprise, and to her annoyance, her tummy fluttered nervously.

"This is Thursday. If you're going to be home on Saturday, Buddy and I will come over and hang out, get Tansy more accustomed to us," he explained. "If we're lucky, she'll slip up and give us a few clues I can use to start putting together a profile to search for her family."

"Oh, I see." Abigail drew in a deep breath, annoyed to realize she'd tensed with anticipation, thinking he might ask her out. "Well, my weekend plans involve yard and house maintenance. It's getting chillier every day and we need to make use of these nice days before winter arrives."

"Then I'll come over and…what? Help rake the leaves off the yard? Put up storm windows?"

She smiled, the friendly, full-wattage brilliance stealing his breath. "Wow, are you actually offering manual labor? Trust me," she said, leaning forward confidingly, "we'll find lots for you to do."

"Why is it I feel as if I just made a huge error in judgment?" he said dryly.

"I have no idea." Her eyes danced with amusement.

"Yeah, right," Quinn muttered.

Quinn walked her back to the library. He watched the sway of her hips as she climbed the steps and disappeared through the door at the top and silently groaned before he turned to cross the street.

"Hey, boss." Karl met him in the outer office. "I could swear I just saw you with Abigail."

"Yeah," Quinn confirmed. His first inclination was to tell Karl to mind his own business, but the deputy's curiosity and obvious speculation made him reconsider. This was a small town. Abby had to live here. He shouldn't stir up gossip. He'd love to get to know her better—a lot better—but that didn't mean Karl had to know it. "She had information about an abandoned child, a little girl."

"No kidding." Karl was instantly all cop.

Quinn left the public area, with its long counter where deputies dealt with citizen requests, and Karl followed him into the inner office.

"How old is she?

"She says she's four and I'd guess that's probably true."

Karl frowned, puzzled. "So she told you her name, address, parents' names, right?"

"Nope." Quinn shrugged out of his leather jacket and slung it over the back of the chair behind the desk.

"She was clearly scared last night when I talked to her and I didn't think it would help to grill her. Plus, she's got Abby on her side. And Abby's pretty adamant that we not question the kid too much."

"Whoa." Karl held up his hands, palms out. "Say no more. That explains everything. If Abby's championing the kid, all the rules go out the window."

"For the moment." Quinn nodded.

"Huh." Karl, hands on hips, contemplated the floor. "So, we've got a genuine mystery to solve."

Quinn grinned at the look of anticipation on his deputy's face. "*I* do," he stressed. "Not you."

"Aw, come on, boss. There's nothing doin' in town but a few drunks I have to roust out of the saloon on Saturday night. This place is dead."

"You've got the burglaries at the ranches," Quinn reminded him.

"Yeah, but I've run into a dead end."

"Sit down and tell me." Quinn pointed at the wooden chair facing his desk.

For the next half hour, he and Karl went over the burglary file. When Karl left to answer a call to assist the highway patrol with a vehicle collision on the highway south of town, Quinn walked with him to the office door.

"Sarah, can you get me the number of the local agency that handles abandoned children?"

"Sure." The dispatcher pulled a phone book from her desk drawer. She shot him a worried glance as she dropped the book on the desktop. "I didn't hear about an abandoned child. Who took the call?"

"I did. Last night." Quinn strolled across the tiled floor and leaned on the counter next to her desk. "Two teenagers dropped a little girl off at Abigail Foster's just as she came home from work."

"Oh." Sarah's brow cleared. "Good to know they had the good sense to pick a safe place. Here we go." She scribbled a number down on a notepad, tore off the sheet and handed it to Quinn.

"Thanks." Quinn went back into his office to make the call. Ten minutes later, he hung up after talking with the social worker and dialed the library.

"Wolf Creek Library." Abigail's voice was professional but warm.

Just like everything else about her, it made him hunger. *Damn, McCloud, get a grip.*

"Abigail, this is Quinn."

"Have you learned something about Tansy?" The hope and concern in her voice was clear.

"I just talked with the social worker and made an appointment for her to talk with you, your aunts and Tansy tonight at six o'clock."

"Where—at the office? Or at our house?"

"At your house."

"Good." Relief filled her voice. "Did you tell her we want to keep her at home with us until her grandmother or father are located?"

"I mentioned you were willing to act as foster parents for the immediate future, while we try to find out where she belongs."

"Okay." She paused. "Will you be there?"

"If you want me to."

"I do. If you're on our side, that is," she said as an afterthought. "You do think Tansy should stay with us, don't you?"

"Absolutely." He felt ridiculously pleased. Everything he'd learned about her told him she was independent and self-contained, yet she'd asked him to help.

She probably only wants you there because you're the sheriff.

Quinn ignored the small voice. He didn't care why she wanted him there—he only cared that she did. And how pathetic was that, he thought with a wry grin.

"I think your house is as good a foster home as she's

likely to get, probably better than most since she's already halfway used to you," he added.

"Oh, excellent. Then we'll see you at six."

Quinn hung up, a half smile curving his lips. *God help that social worker if she gives the Foster women any flak,* he thought. When Abigail set her mind on something, she was a force to be reckoned with.

And apparently she was determined to keep Tansy.

Chapter Six

"Stop fretting." Elizabeth took the dust cloth from Abigail's hand and carried it out to the kitchen. "I dusted the parlor this afternoon. It's clean as can be."

"I'm not fretting," Abigail protested. "I just want the house to be as tidy as possible."

"To impress the social worker? Honey, I've known Cindy Atkins for more than twenty years. She wouldn't notice if we had an inch of dust on the furniture and noseprints all over the windows. The woman never cleans house. And seeing dust in someone else's house isn't on her radar screen."

Abigail laughed. Elizabeth was so practical and reassuring.

"Besides," Elizabeth continued, "I know her supervisor."

Before Abigail could reply, someone rapped on the back door.

"That must be Quinn," she said, hurrying toward the kitchen.

As she crossed the back porch, she could see the shadow of a tall, broad-shouldered man through the curtains. The light over the door outside illuminated both Quinn and Buddy when she pulled open the door.

Oh, my, she thought helplessly. *Shouldn't I be used to how good looking he is by now?* He wore a black T-shirt beneath his bomber jacket and faded jeans covered his long legs. The worn denim clung faithfully to the powerful muscles of his thighs. His black hair gleamed beneath the light, his gray eyes heating, darkening as he swept her from head to foot and back again with a slow, appreciative gaze.

Her heart stuttered and she felt her cheeks heat. His glance had set warmth curling through her abdomen, stirring desires that had lain dormant since her husband died. She knew exactly what her body was telling her and the urge to throw caution to the winds and accept the invitation she read in his eyes was nearly overpowering. But this was neither the time nor the place and besides, Abigail wasn't at all sure she wanted to act on her impulse.

"Come in," she said without greeting, stepping back to wave him inside.

He moved past her and waited, while Buddy trotted into the kitchen. "Is the social worker here yet?"

"No." Abigail walked ahead of him, following Buddy, but when they entered the kitchen, the dog wasn't there and they could hear Tansy's giggles as she greeted the big Lab. Abigail glanced at the clock over the fridge. "She's due any second."

The front door chime rang through the house.

"That must be her."

Quinn followed Abigail down the hall.

Her hips swayed as she walked, the jeans hugging her curves. The thick fall of her hair was dark silk against the white wool of her sweater. She might think the cable turtleneck and jeans were staid, but the clothes hugged her curves and he knew he'd dream about her tonight and what it would be like to peel the sweater and jeans off her and have her naked in his bed. He wondered what kind of underwear she wore, lacy black or plain white.

Not that it mattered, he thought. He was more interested in what she covered with the lingerie.

When they entered the front parlor, Elizabeth and Natasha were standing with a plump middle-aged woman.

"There you are, Quinn," Elizabeth said calmly as she took the woman's coat. "This is Cindy Atkins."

Quinn stepped forward and shook her hand. "We spoke on the phone earlier. Nice to meet you."

"It's a pleasure, Sheriff. I wanted to say hello when

you arrived in town, but I had a late appointment and couldn't be at the welcome meeting."

The garrulous woman didn't give Quinn an opportunity to reply before she continued.

"So I'm glad to have an opportunity to thank you now for agreeing to fill in for poor Sheriff Adams." She glanced at Elizabeth. "Such a shame, his dying so suddenly. I understand he didn't have a history of heart trouble?"

"Not that I'm aware of," Elizabeth replied. "Won't you sit down, Cindy? Quinn, have a seat." Like a general marshaling troops, she soon organized them onto sofa and chairs. "This is Tansy, Cindy."

Quinn had noticed the little girl the moment he'd entered the room. She knelt on the red and cream oriental rug, one arm looped around Buddy's neck, her fingers curled in his fur.

The dog was clearly just as happy to be with Tansy as she was with him. Quinn leaned back in the comfortable wingback chair, anticipating an interesting half hour. He had no doubt Abby and her aunts would win any contest of wills with the chatty social worker. He didn't know how determined the woman might be to enforce the department rules, but if there was a difference of opinion about Tansy's welfare, he'd put his money on Abby winning.

"Hello there." Cindy smiled at the little girl. "Who's your friend?"

"His name's Buddy. He belongs to Quinn."

"Ah, I see. Well, then." Cindy looked at Quinn, then at Abigail and her aunts. "Perhaps we should begin with the adults and then I'll talk to Tansy?" She slipped a pad of paper and several forms from her briefcase at her feet. "Let's start with you, Abigail."

One by one, the adults gave abbreviated versions of the events of the last twenty-four hours. Quinn quietly observed Tansy.

By the time the social worker finished questioning Quinn, Tansy had nestled next to Abby in the big chair. Buddy sat in front of her, his head against her knees. Abby's arm tucked around the little girl.

Quinn felt a surge of warmth and admiration for both Abby and the child wise enough to instinctively seek out the woman most likely to fight to protect her.

Not that the aunts wouldn't protect her as well, he thought, but Abby seemed to feel some kind of right to first claim on Tansy since she'd been the one to find her.

"We've all assured Tansy that we'll keep her safe until her father arrives to get her," he said to the social worker. "We're hoping you'll help us do that by approving Abby and her aunts as temporary foster parents. She's settled here and already attached to Abby. It's not in anyone's interests to move her at this point."

"There are forms to be filled out, and procedures to follow," Cindy said. "But we can place Tansy here in an emergency foster care situation while we wait for approval."

Cindy turned to Quinn. "If the sheriff's office will back me up, I'm willing to approve the Foster home as an urgent-need foster home."

"My office will," Quinn said firmly, without a moment's hesitation.

"Then I believe we have a solution," Cindy said. Her voice was brisk as she continued. "I'll just need the four of you to sign the forms."

Within a half hour, the social worker was on her way, forms signed approving Tansy's remaining in the care of Abigail and her aunts.

"Whew." Abigail closed the door and sagged against it. "Thanks," she told Quinn, who stood in the foyer with her.

"Glad to help." He eyed her. "I'm not sure you needed me, though. You and your aunts are a formidable team."

"Having you add the weight of the sheriff's office made it easier for her to agree."

He shrugged. "Maybe. Bottom line is, the kid needs somewhere to stay while I look for her family and she might as well stay here. Doesn't make sense to ship her off to a strange place."

"That's something we can agree on." Abigail pushed away from the door at the sound of a thud and Buddy's deep bark in the parlor. "I'd better see what's going on in there."

"Maybe I'd better take Buddy home before he gets Tansy in trouble."

She laughed and they headed for the parlor.

Quinn and Buddy left for home and Tansy spent the rest of the evening explaining the inside jokes on her favorite Disney sitcom to Elizabeth and Natasha. Abigail and the little girl left the great-aunts reading in the front parlor when it was Tansy's bedtime.

"Do I get to stay with you, and Miss Elizabeth and Miss Natasha?" the little girl asked as they climbed the stairs.

Abigail looked down. Tansy's thick-lashed blue eyes held an expression of hope mixed with worry.

"Yes, you do." Abigail nodded firmly. "You're going to stay with us until your dad comes to get you."

"My daddy's going to come get me soon," Tansy said solemnly.

"All right." Abigail nodded. "When your daddy arrives, you'll be waiting for him, okay?"

"Okay." Relief washed over the childish face in a wave, her expression lightening with intense relief. "I'm glad," she confided.

A half hour later, bathed and tucked into clean pajamas, Tansy sat with Abigail on the bed. Their backs against the headboard, legs stretched out in front of them, Tansy hovered over Abigail's lap as they read a chapter from the well-worn and much-loved copy of a tale of Eloise and her friends at New York City's Plaza Hotel.

"Time to turn the lights out," Abigail said when she glanced down and saw Tansy struggling to hold her eyes open.

"No, no. Please, can't we read just a few more pages?" she protested.

"Tomorrow," Abigail promised. "You need to get lots of rest tonight. We have a busy day tomorrow. Before the social worker left earlier, Elizabeth promised she'd take you to preschool and register you tomorrow."

"Do I have to start school tomorrow?" Tansy said, worrying her lower lip and looking anxious.

"No, we'll get you registered but you won't be starting until Monday. I think we need to go shopping and find some pretty outfits for you first. Will you like that?"

"Yes." Tansy smiled, blue eyes sparkling.

"Good." Abigail stood and slipped the book back on its shelf. Tansy slid lower on the bed, her head on the pillow, and Abigail pulled up the covers, tucking them under her chin. "'Night, sleep tight."

"'Night," Tansy murmured, her eyes already drifting closed.

Abigail stood for a few moments, looking down at the small form in the bed. Tansy's face with its pointed chin, high cheekbones and Cupid's bow mouth was framed in a fan of brown hair against the white pillowcase. The vulnerability in the small features caught at Abigail's heart. She brushed a silky strand of brown hair from the childish cheek and tiptoed out of the room, easing the door nearly closed. She left it ajar just enough to allow the soft glow of the night-light in the bathroom across the hall to illuminate the room faintly. If Tansy woke, Abigail didn't want her to be afraid in the dark.

On Saturday morning, Quinn woke early. By six-thirty, he let himself and Buddy out of the apartment and jogged down the steps.

"Come here, Bud." The big dog loped near and sat while Quinn clipped a leash on his collar.

Then the two set off down the alley to the street. It was chilly enough for Quinn to see each breath he expelled and he was glad he'd pulled on a thick hooded sweatshirt before leaving the apartment. His leg ached but the stretching he'd done earlier had loosened and warmed the muscles enough to make the pain bearable.

He jogged the blocks through downtown, running down residential sidewalks for forty minutes, then stopped at Elsie's café and got a cup of coffee before slowing to a fast walk to cool down on the way home. Buddy veered toward the open park several blocks from his apartment and Quinn stopped, snapping the leash free of his collar to let him run. While Quinn cut across the park on one of the walkways that made a big X from corner to corner and divided the park into quarter sections, Buddy zigzagged across the lawn, nose to the ground.

They reached the alley leading home barely an hour after they'd left and as they climbed the steps to the apartment, Quinn saw Abigail walk past the window in her kitchen. Her hair was caught up in a ponytail and she wore a light gray sweatshirt. She turned to speak to someone and Tansy walked into view, took a mug from Abigail's hand and the two disappeared.

"She acts like that kid's mama," Quinn told Buddy. The Lab pricked his ears and cocked his head to the side, as if listening with interest. "Hope it doesn't break her heart when the real parent shows up."

He loped up the stairs, Buddy at his heels, and headed for the shower. He'd promised to help the Foster women with yard work today and damned if he wasn't looking forward to it.

As if raking her leaves is going to get you laid, McCloud, he thought with self-derision. The mere thought of getting naked with Abigail made him itch with frustration.

By 10:00 a.m., Quinn had raked leaves from the lawn and flower beds in both the front and back yards of the big old Victorian house. Abigail finished spreading mulch over flower beds in the front and joined him when he started raking the sideyard.

"I think you're losing ground," Elizabeth called from the back step.

Abigail and Quinn looked up from the growing pile of leaves next to the white picket fence that separated the Fosters' side yard from the neighbor next door.

Elizabeth smiled at their blank expressions and pointed toward the backyard where the big maple tree stood.

"Oh, no," Abigail said with consternation.

Quinn leaned on his rake, grinning at Tansy and Buddy. Buddy rolled in the big pile of leaves under the maple tree while Tansy struggled unsuccessfully to stop him as he scattered the red and gold leaves across the newly raked lawn. While the adults watched, Buddy jumped up and licked Tansy's face, knocking her backward into the soft leaves.

She shrieked with laughter, covering her face and giggling as the dog stood over her, tail wagging, and tried enthusiastically to lick her again.

"Buddy," Quinn called. "Leave her alone."

The dog looked over his shoulder, spied Quinn and abandoned the little girl, galloping straight toward Abigail, who was laughing at his antics.

"Look out." Quinn dropped his rake and reached for Abby, who turned to run.

Too late. Buddy barreled into Abby, knocking her forward into Quinn. Instinctively Quinn wrapped his arms around her and went over backward, landing on his back with Abby on top of him. Buddy barked with excitement and nosed Abigail's hair, trying to lick her face.

"Stop that, Buddy," Quinn ordered, shouldering the big dog aside as he rolled and tucked Abigail safely beneath him. She was breathless from laughter.

"Come here, Buddy!" Tansy called. The dog's ears lifted and he turned to race back across the lawn and join the little girl in the pile of leaves.

"This is chaos." Quinn's voice was raspy with mirth.

"That dog of yours is out of control," Abigail said. She was heart-poundingly aware of the length of his body stretched over hers, his weight blanketing her.

"Yeah. I'm thinking he needs to go back to puppy school," Quinn told her, his mouth lifting at the corners.

"I'm not sure it's possible to rake the lawn today," she told him. She really should push him away and get up. What would her aunts think? But the flex and shift of the hard length of his thighs against hers as he twisted to look over his shoulder at Buddy sent heat racing through her veins. She fought the urge to press closer.

"Oh, we can rake it," he responded dryly. "We just can't get the leaves off the ground."

Elizabeth's voice joined Tansy's and Quinn chuckled. "I'm not sure even your great-aunt can control those two. Tansy and Buddy love playing in the piles."

He looked back at Abby, his gaze meeting hers, and heat flared in his gray eyes. The curve of his mouth turned sensual. He lowered his head and nuzzled her throat, burying his face in her hair just below her ear. "Damn, you smell good."

"So do you." Every breath she took drew in his scent and sent her nerves humming. She loved the way he smelled. She dragged in a deeper breath and burrowed closer.

The impact of what she was doing, what she was feeling, slammed into her and she stiffened.

Uh-oh. This can't be happening. No way.

She flattened her palms against his chest and pushed.

"What?" Reluctantly, he lifted his face from the soft skin of her throat and looked down at her.

"This has to stop. I am *so* not going there."

"Huh?" Confusion filled his eyes.

"Human behavioral studies have proven that pheremones emitted by males attract specific women. Regardless of sensible, intelligent reasons why the two won't suit, their bodies give off scents that fuse them together like rabbits."

He grinned, amusement lighting his eyes. "Well, I'll be damned. So you think that's why I can't keep my hands off you—you're zapping me with female hormones? And I'm zapping you with mine?"

"Laugh all you want." She shoved at him and he rolled to the side, still grinning. "But this—" she waved her hand between their two bodies "—isn't going to happen."

"Oh, yeah," he said, his deep voice raspy with arousal. "It is. Bet on it."

"No, it's not." She jumped to her feet and brushed down her shirt and jeans. "We know what's causing it and we can refuse to go there."

He rose easily to his feet and bent to murmur in her ear, "But I want to."

Heat flushed her entire body. *So do I.* "We're adults. We both know we can't have everything we want."

He cupped her cheek in one big, warm hand. She closed her eyes against the instant need to lean into his touch.

"I agree we're both adults. Single, unattached adults. There's no reason I'm aware of that making love would harm anyone. How about you?"

"It could harm us," she said without thinking.

"I'd never harm you, honey. I'll only bite if you want me to."

She froze, stunned by the swift, carnal, mental image his words painted in her brain.

Then she shook it off and stepped back. His hand fell away.

"I don't sleep around," she said. "For a good reason. Being intimate with a man isn't casual for me—my heart gets involved. And I don't want my heart involved with a man who's only going to be around temporarily. You'll leave. And I'll be…upset. So let's stop this before anything gets started."

Hands on hips, he stared at her, his eyes unreadable. "All right. I don't agree with you but I'll try to leave you alone. But if you start anything, I'll finish it." He leaned down until their noses nearly touched. "And just for the record, I don't believe for a minute either one of us is going to be able to ignore this. I want you. You want me. Your brain may tell you to ignore what's going on between us, but your brain's wrong. When you realize how crazy it is to ignore something this strong, you're going to regret holding out and wasting time we could have spent enjoying each other."

Abigail glared at him but she didn't tell him he was

wrong. First, because all her energy was required to keep from grabbing him and pulling his mouth the few inches to hers. And second, because she was afraid he was right.

She'd finally met a man who appealed to her on such a basic, male-female level that she wasn't at all sure her intellectual strength was capable of overruling her body's demands.

Added to that, her heart melted every time she watched him handle Tansy with gentleness or affectionately rub Buddy's ears. There was no denying both child and dog adored him. And Abigail was well on her way to making them a threesome.

He turned and walked away, joining Tansy and Buddy. He ordered Buddy to sit a few feet away from the decimated pile of leaves and began to rake. Tansy helped by carrying armfuls of leaves to deposit on the growing new pile.

The air was crisp, but everyone agreed that the sunshine, which would soon give way to snowier, colder days, was too precious to waste by going inside. So once the leaves had been conquered, they gathered on the porch for tea.

Tansy curled up on the rattan couch and accepted a cup of warm apple cider from Elizabeth. She blew on the hot liquid, spitting with earnestness as she did so.

Quinn hid a grin and watched the little girl take a hesitant sip of the cider.

Meanwhile, Elizabeth poured steaming hot tea into

a delicate white cup and held it out to him. "Sugar?" she asked, reaching for the bowl.

"No, thank you," he answered, awkwardly taking the china cup. It felt ridiculously small and fragile in his hand. His fingers wouldn't fit through the handle, so he cradled it in his palm, his fingers wrapping around it.

Abigail accepted a cup from Elizabeth, a lemon slice gently moving on the surface of the fragrant tea. "Not a tea drinker, Quinn?" she asked, clearly amused.

He lifted the cup and took a drink, swallowing and grimacing as the hot liquid slid down his throat. "No. More of a beer and burger guy."

Tansy sat up at the mention of a burger. "Oooh, I love cheeseburgers. They're my absolutest favorite thing to eat."

"I knew you were a smart kid," Quinn replied, grinning at Tansy.

The little girl glowed, clearly soaking up Quinn's compliment. "I love McDonald's, but my mommy likes Dick's better," she said, licking her lips.

"Dick? Is that a neighbor friend, Tansy?" Abigail asked casually, careful to keep her tone light.

"Nope," Tansy answered, slurping her cider.

"Tansy, you wouldn't be talking about Dick's Drive-In, would you?" Quinn asked as he stroked Buddy's ears.

The little girl finished her cider and set the cup down on the seat next to her. "Yep, you can sit in your car and eat. Isn't that super cool?"

Quinn grinned at Tansy and nodded his head, then swept the aunts and Abby with a glance. "I have to vote with Tansy. There's a Dick's Drive-In not far from my apartment in Seattle. If I want a great burger, that's where I go."

Tansy's eyes grew big with astonishment. "You live in Seattle, too?"

"Yeah, I do."

"What are you doing here?"

"I'm working," Quinn told her. "Just for a while. Then I'm going back to Seattle. How about you?"

"I'm not working." Tansy grinned at him, her eyes gleaming with laughter. "I'm too little to work."

"Yes, but you go to preschool," Elizabeth put in.

"She starts on Monday," Abby added, looking at Quinn.

Natasha offered the plate of sugar cookies to Tansy and chuckled when the little girl took two. "I think all this talk of burgers has given you an appetite."

Quinn took a cookie from Natasha's plate, shoved back his chair and stood, Buddy following suit. "Thanks for the tea, ladies. It's time for me to head out," he said. "I need to check in at the office."

The look he gave the women said he was on his way to the station to check out the Seattle lead.

Abigail shivered as the breeze picked up and the sun was obscured behind a cloud. "And I think it's about time that a certain little girl had a bath."

Tansy looked around at all of the adults, then turned

to Buddy. "I think she means you, stinky dog!" She giggled as the dog's ears lifted and his tail wagged with enthusiasm.

"I said girl, not dog. C'mon, you, I'll let you use the lavender bubble bath."

"Okay, I guess." Tansy stood and walked toward the door. "Bye, Quinn. Bye, my Buddy!"

The big dog slurped the little girl's face as she walked by him, then padded down the steps after Quinn.

"I'll talk to you all later," Quinn called over his shoulder, his tone telling the women that he'd check in if he found anything in Seattle.

"I forgot to ask Quinn something," Abigail said, standing quickly. "Elizabeth, would you start Tansy's bath? I'll only be a few minutes."

"Sure. Come on, kiddo, let's head upstairs." Elizabeth held the door open for the little girl as Abigail ran lightly down the steps, following Quinn around the side yard to the back.

Quinn was halfway across the lawn to the apartment when she reached the rear of the house.

"Quinn, wait."

He looked over his shoulder and stopped, turning to face her. "What's up?"

"I just wanted to ask if you think knowing Tansy once lived in Seattle means you can find her father," Abigail said as she joined him.

Quinn shrugged. "No way of knowing. Smith is a

common name. It's going to take some serious footwork to get any information on a child. She won't be in the databases we normally use to find adults."

"Like what?"

"Like the state driver's license department," he said patiently. "Or the judicial system. That's usually the easiest way to get a hit on an adult because those two departments have a huge database made up of a wide cross section of adults."

"I see." Abigail bit her lip. "I'd hoped knowing that she'd lived in Seattle would make it easier."

"Every piece of information helps," he told her. "But so far, we don't have anything that would make me tell you I'm certain the search is going to be easy."

Abigail's shoulder slumped. "I was so hoping…" she murmured, almost to herself.

"I know." Quinn wrapped his arms around her and pulled her close, cradling her against the heat and comfort of his body. "But the good news is, she doesn't seem anxious about being found. I have to assume she's right when she told you her dad is in the military and will come get her."

"I hope you're right."

They stood still for a moment, his much bigger body sheltering hers. Abigail slowly became aware of a gathering tension in the powerful muscles she pressed against and the arms that wrapped around her. Sexual awareness flooded her and she stepped back, his arms falling away.

"Thank you," she said unsteadily. The brooding heat in his eyes as he watched her made her nerves hum with warning.

She glanced around. They were alone in the back-yard, with no neighbors visible on either side.

"I should let you go." She glanced down at herself and shook her head. Grasping the distraction, she brushed leaves and twigs from her jeans and sweater, shaking her hair and combing her fingers through the long strands to free small leaves. "I'm still covered in leaf debris," she protested with a shaky, small laugh. "I don't think I can get it out without a shower and shampoo."

Quinn slipped an arm around her waist and tugged her back until her shoulder blades were against his chest, her thighs resting against the rock-hard muscles of his.

"Come to my apartment. I'll help you scrub. I'll rinse the leaves out of your hair." His deep voice was seduction itself, murmuring into her ear.

For one glorious moment, she let herself lean against him, his strength supporting her. Then she forced her feet to step away and she turned to face him. "No, thanks."

"Why not?" He brushed his lips over her throat, just below her ear.

Abigail's eyes drifted closed. She was so tempted.

"You only want me because I've said no," she managed to get out. "That's really what's behind your determination to get me into bed. I've seen your résumé—you thrive on challenges."

Quinn went still. Not a muscle moved, but Abigail felt as if he loomed larger.

He released her, stepping back as she turned to face him.

His features were all the more dangerous for their total lack of expression.

"You read my résumé?"

"Yes," she said warily.

"Before we met?"

Even his voice was flat. The lack of inflection in his words echoed the zero expression on his features.

"Yes." She watched his gray eyes go icy. "I shouldn't have. I wouldn't normally have had access to it, but Elizabeth is on the town council. She left papers out on the dining room table and when I cleared them, your résumé was on top. It listed your assignments over the last several years—I couldn't help but see it."

"So now we know why you don't want anything to do with me."

Quinn didn't move, but Abigail felt his retreat as if he'd stepped back even farther.

"What do you mean?" she asked, bewildered.

He glanced over her shoulder and pursed his lips. The sharp whistle had Buddy bounding toward them.

"Quinn, I didn't mean to invade your privacy...." Instinctively, she lifted her hand to catch his forearm but froze when his gaze met hers. His was impersonal and pure ice; he looked right through her.

"I don't give a damn about privacy. See you around, Abigail."

And he turned and walked away.

Abigail wasn't sure what had just happened, but she was positive that somehow, without meaning to, she'd deeply insulted Quinn.

And she cared about him—too much to ever hurt him, she realized with sudden clarity.

Abigail heard Quinn's truck leave early Sunday morning and lay awake that night until she heard him come home around eleven-thirty. She wondered where he'd spent the day and couldn't help wondering, too, if he was avoiding her.

Unable to sleep, she stared at the window where moonlight made shadowy patterns through the lace curtains. What was it about Quinn McCloud that made her want to run in the opposite direction?

The physical pull between them was powerful, she knew. But she'd been physically attracted to her husband without this element of instinctive caution. Was it only because Quinn would be leaving when the town hired a permanent sheriff? Or that his career had put him in dangerous places and left him with the skills to deal with violence?

She frowned. No, there was more to her reluctance than that. His protectiveness toward Tansy and his respectful kindness toward her aunts demonstrated without words that he was a good man. Still, something about him made her feel…unsettled.

Perhaps it was because he disturbed the quiet tenor of the life she loved. She'd been twenty-two when Manny died, and losing her husband after a few short months of marriage had broken her heart. She still didn't know how she'd managed to finish her senior year and graduate, but she did know that returning to Wolf Creek had provided a haven she'd desperately needed. The calm, even flow of small-town life had saved her sanity when grief had threatened to destroy her. Six years later, she wasn't sure she wanted anything to change.

Even when change might have arrived in the undeniably attractive male package that was Quinn.

Quinn called the Foster house and left a message with Elizabeth around noon on Monday. So far, his queries in Seattle hadn't resulted in any new information about the identity or whereabouts of Tansy's father or grandmother.

He could just as easily have telephoned Abigail at work, or walked across the street to the library and told her in person.

But the truth was, he didn't want to talk to her. He didn't want to hear in her voice, or see in her face when she looked at him, confirmation that she couldn't deal with his past.

He didn't know why it mattered. Other women had shrunk away from him, or cozied up with avid eyes when they learned he'd killed in the line of duty. He'd never cared before.

But for some reason, knowing his past mattered to Abigail bothered him. He didn't want to think about why.

Fortunately for Quinn's peace of mind, the usually quiet office picked up its pace in the afternoon. He stayed busy with two fender-benders on county roads followed by a rancher reporting three missing steers. It was after 9:00 p.m. before he returned to Wolf Creek and nearly ten before he finished eating a steak at the restaurant and headed for his truck.

"Damn." The police radio clipped to his belt chirped its alarm. He lifted it, thumbing the on switch just as he reached his truck and pulled open the driver's door. "McCloud here. What's up?"

"A fight at the Creek Street Tavern."

"Is Karl still out on the domestic violence call?"

"He finished and is on his way back to town. Estimates twenty minutes before he reaches city limits."

"All right. I'll take the tavern call. Tell Karl to meet me there."

Quinn signed off and climbed into his truck.

"For a quiet town, this place has had a helluva busy day," he grumbled as he waited for a dark green, four-wheel-drive pickup to drive past. The truck had a McCloud Ranch logo on the door panels and the driver lifted his hand. Quinn returned the greeting automatically before recognizing Chase McCloud.

The Reader Service—Here's how it works:

Accepting your 2 free books and 2 free mystery gifts (gifts are worth about $10.00) places you under no obligation to buy anything. You may keep the books and gifts and return the shipping statement marked "cancel." If you do not cancel, about a month later we'll send you 6 additional books and bill you just $4.24 each in the U.S. or $4.99 each in Canada. That's a savings of 15% off the cover price. It's quite a bargain! Shipping and handling is just 50¢ per book.* You may cancel at any time, but if you choose to continue, every month we'll send you 6 more books, which you may either purchase at the discount price or return to us and cancel your subscription.

*Terms and prices subject to change without notice. Prices do not include applicable taxes. Sales tax applicable in N.Y. Canadian residents will be charged applicable provincial taxes and GST. Offer not valid in Quebec. All orders subject to approval. Credit or debit balances in a customer's account(s) may be offset by any other outstanding balance owed by or to the customer. Please allow 4 to 6 weeks for delivery. Offer available while quantities last.

If offer card is missing write to: The Reader Service, P.O. Box 1867, Buffalo, NY 14240-1867 or visit us at www.ReaderService.com.

NO POSTAGE
NECESSARY
IF MAILED
IN THE
UNITED STATES

BUSINESS REPLY MAIL

FIRST-CLASS MAIL   PERMIT NO. 717   BUFFALO, NY

POSTAGE WILL BE PAID BY ADDRESSEE

THE READER SERVICE
PO BOX 1867
BUFFALO NY 14240-9952

Play the Lucky Hearts Game

and get...
2 FREE BOOKS and
2 FREE Mystery GIFTS...
YOURS to KEEP!

yes! I have scratched off the gold card.
Please send me my *2 FREE BOOKS* and
2 FREE Mystery GIFTS (gifts are worth about $10).
I understand that I am under no obligation to purchase
any books as explained on the back of this card.

Scratch Here!
Then look below to see what your
cards get you...*2 Free Books
& 2 Free Mystery Gifts!*

We want to make sure we offer you the best service suited to your needs. Please answer the
following question:
About how many NEW paperback fiction books have you purchased in the past 3 months?
❏ 0-2 ❏ 3-6 ❏ 7 or more

335 SDL EZLW 235 SDL EZL9

FIRST NAME LAST NAME

ADDRESS

APT. CITY

Visit us online at
www.ReaderService.com

STATE / PROV. ZIP/POSTAL CODE

Twenty-one gets you
2 FREE BOOKS and
2 FREE MYSTERY GIFTS!

Twenty gets you
2 FREE BOOKS!

Nineteen gets you
1 FREE BOOK!

TRY AGAIN!

Offer limited to one per household and not valid to current subscribers of Silhouette Special Edition® books. **Your Privacy—**
Silhouette Books is committed to protecting your privacy. Our Privacy Policy is available online at www.eHarlequin.com or upon
request from the Reader Service. From time to time we make our lists of customers available to reputable third parties who may
have a product or service of interest to you. If you would prefer for us not to share your name and address, please check here ❏.

Help us get it right—We strive for accurate, respectful and relevant communications. To clarify or modify your communication
preferences, visit us at www.ReaderService.com/consumerschoice.

▼ **DETACH AND MAIL CARD TODAY!** ▼

® and ™ are trademarks owned and used by the trademark owner and/or its licensee

© 2009 HARLEQUIN ENTERPRISES LIMITED. Printed in the U.S.A.

(S-SE-09/09)

As soon as Chase's truck was out of the way, Quinn spun the steering wheel, executing a U-turn in the middle of the block and heading for Creek Street. He'd just passed the first cross street when headlights appeared in his rearview mirror. Then they switched off, the vehicle following close behind him.

Frowning, Quinn narrowed his eyes. He recognized the dark green truck.

He pulled into the tavern's gravel parking lot and stepped out, closing the door with a quiet thunk. Chase pulled in beside him and got out, tucking a handgun into his waistband at the small of his back. The denim jacket he wore concealed the weapon.

"What are you doing here?" Quinn demanded.

Chase grinned. "All the McCloud vehicles have police scanners—I heard the call." He jerked his chin toward the tavern door. "Figured you could use some backup until Karl gets here."

"You're not deputized," Quinn said.

"But I can make a citizen's arrest, if I need to," Chase shot back.

Quinn shook his head. "Are all you McClouds crazy?"

"Pretty much."

"Hell." Quinn gave in. "All right. But if Ren hears you're freelancing, you're taking the heat."

"He knows. He told me to look after you. Besides, you're a McCloud."

Quinn froze, his eyes narrowing. "So we have the same last name. So what?"

Chase shrugged, his eyes unreadable. "While you're in Wolf Creek, we've got your back. That's all I'm sayin'."

Quinn had a gut feeling there was more behind Chase's blunt declaration. But if the big rancher suspected they shared more than a surname, he wasn't saying. And Quinn didn't have time, nor the inclination, to question him further. Regardless of why Chase had volunteered, Quinn was glad to have his help. He'd think about just what their conversation meant later, after they'd cleared out the bar.

He turned and headed for the tavern entrance, Chase on his heels.

Chapter Seven

Tuesday night, Quinn met Karl at the Wolf Creek Saloon at seven-thirty. The poolroom was in back, through an archway separating it from the main room. The uncomplicated camaraderie of shooting pool with the guys was a welcome respite from work—and the thoughts of Abby that haunted him. Quinn was bent over the table and made a shot that tapped the five ball into the side pocket when two men paused in the archway.

Quinn glanced up and saw them as they headed toward him.

"Hey, Luke, Zach." He leaned over, took a second shot and missed. Karl took his place and Quinn walked to the nearby waist-high table, picked up his beer and took a seat on one of the tall stools. "What's up?"

Luke shrugged. "Not much."

"We're free men tonight. The wives are out at Mom's place, planning a baby shower for Raine," Zach said, grinning when Karl snorted.

"If you weren't married, you'd be free every night," the younger man pointed out.

"Yeah, but we'd sleep alone," Luke drawled.

"Not always," Karl shot back.

"Son." Zach clapped a hand on Karl's shoulder. "If you marry the right woman, it's worth it."

Quinn had an instant mental image of just how Abigail would look after being kissed, her eyes drowsy, lips swollen. He slammed the door on the picture and tipped his beer bottle to drink.

"I've got a twenty-dollar bill that says I can take you guys, best three out of four," Karl announced.

Quinn realized he'd missed the intervening conversation.

"You're on," Luke said, selecting a cue from the rack on the nearby wall.

Karl and Luke argued good-naturedly as Karl racked the pool balls. Zach left them to it and joined Quinn at the table.

"How's it going at the office?" Zach said. "You settling in okay?"

Quinn shrugged. "It's been fairly quiet. There was a

bar brawl at the Creek Street Tavern last night. Chase happened to be in town and helped me arrest a couple guys, but other than that, not a lot happening."

"Wolf Creek isn't exactly a hotbed of crime, but it has its moments," Zach commented. "Who did you arrest at the tavern?"

Quinn gave him a couple of names and Zach laughed.

"I should have known," he said. "Those two start a fight at the tavern at least once a month. Are they still in jail?"

"Nah, I let them go when they sobered up. They'll probably be charged with disturbing the peace."

"At least nobody went to the hospital," Zach said dryly. He grinned at Quinn. "I'm guessing your last job was a little more exciting, eh?"

"My last job ended with a bullet in my leg," Quinn told him.

"Chase mentioned you'd been shot." Zach looked down. "Which leg, right or left?"

"Left." Quinn automatically rubbed the ever-present ache in his upper thigh. "Still hurts but it's getting better."

"Man, I hate getting shot." Zach shook his head and grimaced.

Quinn lifted an eyebrow in silent query and the other man explained.

"I was military for years—probably still would be if it hadn't been for my grandfather dying and leaving half his property to my sister, mom and me."

Quinn nodded slowly, eyes narrowing in thought.

"Seems I heard something about that from Ren—wasn't there some trouble with an uncle, or a cousin, about the will and how the property was divided?"

Zach's face hardened. "Harlan and Lonnie Kerrigan. Yeah, I think you could say there was some trouble. They're both in jail—hopefully for a long time."

Quinn whistled, a low, almost silent sound. "So now you're responsible for all the family property left by your granddad? I can see why you left the military."

"I manage the section my family inherited," Zach corrected. "Harlan still owns a chunk of land in this county—some left to him by Granddad and some he acquired afterward."

"How's he operating it from behind bars?" Quinn asked, curious.

"As far as I can tell, he isn't." Zach's disgust was plain. "There's a foreman living at the headquarters of the main ranch, but the fences and buildings are going to hell."

Quinn shrugged. "What goes around, comes around. Sounds like your uncle is getting payback."

"Maybe. It's a damn shame to see the land go to waste like that, though." Zach tilted his bottle, drank and eyed Quinn. "Chase tells me you worked cattle, back when you were a kid."

"Yeah," Quinn said absently, watching as Karl slammed the six ball into an end pocket and whooped with satisfaction. "Down in New Mexico."

"Nice country." Zach's voice was mild. "A lot more

mountains than we've got here. I went hiking there with a friend once, years ago, down near the Mexican border. Then we spent a few days in Santa Fe."

"Nice town," Quinn agreed.

"We had a good time—with a blonde and a brunette, if I remember right," Zach said with a grin. "Did you live in that part of New Mexico when you were a kid?"

Quinn didn't move so much as a muscle, but he was suddenly aware that Zach was grilling him. His questions weren't casual—he was trying to get information. Quinn tipped his bottle and drank, considering how much to tell him.

"No, I cowboy'd in Billy the Kid country." He turned his head and met Zach's eyes with a challenging stare. "I grew up in Texas, near Austin, left home when I was sixteen and wound up working in New Mexico. I'm guessing you were born and raised in Wolf Creek."

Zach's wry smile acknowledged Quinn knew his questions weren't casual. "You'd be right. Left here and enlisted in the military as soon as I was out of high school."

Zach didn't ask Quinn any more questions about his childhood, but by the time they all left the saloon, having spent the better part of three hours shooting pool and swapping stories, Quinn headed for home convinced the McCloud clan suspected he was one of them.

He knew there was little chance they'd have their suspicions confirmed, not unless he gave them the information. His birth parents were never married. His original birth certificate listed "Sean McCloud" as his biological father, but the certificate had been reissued when he was two years old and his mother's new husband, Leonard Kennedy, adopted him. The adoption files were sealed. Kennedy resented his wife's child; he and Quinn disliked each other intensely. At eighteen, Quinn filed with the court to gain access to his adoption records, learn his real father's name and have his own surname changed to match.

Nope, he thought as he lay in bed, staring at the ceiling. The McClouds might wonder but they'd never be sure he was a member of the family—not unless he decided to tell them. And he still didn't know if he wanted to do that. After dealing with Leonard Kennedy's heavy-handed use of a belt to enforce his commands and the absentminded parenting of his mother, Quinn had few illusions about family. Experience told him he was better off on his own.

Just out of curiosity, though, he decided to drive out to the McCloud Ranch and pay a visit to John and Margaret McCloud. Though it had been over a week since the burglary on the night he arrived, he could easily use the pretext of questioning them about the robbery to explain his visit.

The following morning, he left the office around ten and headed out of Wolf Creek.

Following Sarah's directions, Quinn located the big mailbox with McCloud Ranch lettered on the side and turned off the highway, drove beneath a wrought-iron arch and down a graveled lane. The road ran between fenced pastures where purebred whiteface Hereford cattle and blooded quarter horses grazed.

He pulled up in front of the house and got out, one swift glance sweeping the ranch yard where barns, outbuildings and corrals sat in a half circle with the house facing them.

The big house sat in a square of lawn and flower beds, trimmed and apparently ready for winter. Quinn unlatched the wrought-iron gate and closed it behind him before heading up the flagstone path to the front door. Water fell and splashed somewhere nearby, the sound reaching him as he waited for someone to answer. He wondered idly if the water, he assumed from a fountain, froze in the winter.

The carved, heavy wooden door swung inward.

"Yes?" The auburn-haired woman in the doorway was dressed in a deep green shirt and cream wool slacks. Gold gleamed at her earlobes, on her fingers and wrist. She looked expensive.

"Morning, ma'am." Quinn pulled off his sunglasses, guessing the woman was probably Margaret McCloud. "I'm Quinn McCloud, acting sheriff in Wolf Creek."

"Of course." A smile broke over the woman's face and she beamed at him. "Come in, come in." She waved him inside and closed the door. "John and I were just having morning coffee. I'm Margaret McCloud." She led the way down a hall.

Quinn caught a glimpse of a huge living room with leather chairs and sofa, Western artwork and family photos.

"John, this is our new sheriff."

The big man sitting at the island counter in the sunny kitchen stood, leaning across the counter to shake Quinn's hand.

"We were out of town and missed the get-together last week," he said. "Have a seat."

Quinn laid his sunglasses on the countertop and slid onto the tall stool. Margaret set a mug in front of him and poured coffee while John pushed a plate of cookies nearer.

"How's everything going with the job? Pretty quiet in town?"

"Wolf Creek's quiet, but we've had a few burglaries, breaking and entering, on surrounding ranches when the owners are out of town. Actually, that's why I'm here." He took a sip of coffee. "The first night I arrived, there was a burglary at the Nelson place—I'm making the rounds of the neighbors to find out if they saw or heard anything out of the ordinary."

"Not that I remember." John frowned, glancing at his wife. "What about you, Margaret? Have you heard anything about it?"

"Susan called and told me about the break-in just before we left for Helena. I think it was the day after it happened. But no one seems to know anything." She looked at Quinn. "Every now and then, a group of teenagers will do something like this. But usually one of them talks and the word gets out, then the parents make restitution. But this time, all the usual suspects appear to be innocent, unless they're just not talking." She shook her head. "We have very little serious crime in our community. It's very worrisome to actually be having criminal activity."

The conversation turned to general discussion of Wolf Creek and its residents. By the time Quinn drove away an hour later, he still wasn't sure whether John suspected there was a family connection between them. But he was sure he genuinely liked the friendly couple, just as he liked Chase and the rest of the McClouds.

Wednesday evening Abigail tucked Tansy into bed for the night and left the house. She crossed the back lawn and climbed the stairs to the apartment over the garage with trepidation. She owed Quinn an apology. She'd caught only brief glimpses of him since their last conversation and he hadn't called to tell her the results of his attempted search for Tansy through Seattle authorities. Instead, he'd telephoned Elizabeth. That had been confirmation enough that she'd done something to hurt him.

Which was ridiculous, she told herself, because Quinn McCloud seemed to have the tough hide of a rhinoceros. He had the aura of a quintessential tough guy who would scorn anything remotely emotional or touchy-feely.

Still, she couldn't stop feeling as if she'd made a bad error in judgment.

So I'll apologize and if he doesn't want to accept my apology, that's his problem. I'll have done my part.

She reached the landing at the top of the stairs. The rhythmic thump of rock music was audible, confirming that Quinn was awake. Abigail drew a deep breath and knocked on the door.

The music level decreased and a second later the door opened.

Abigail's eyes widened and her prepared speech flew right out of her head.

Quinn stood in the open doorway wearing jogging shorts, his chest bare. Perspiration beaded his brow and sheened the powerful muscles of his shoulders, arms, chest and abs. His thighs were roped with muscle below the hem of the gray knit shorts, but an ugly scar marred the left one. Barely healed, based on the appearance of still-red skin.

There were other scars as well, but their outlines were white, clearly older.

"Do you need something, Abby?"

His deep voice, the words polite but emotionless, broke the spell that bound her and she nodded, dragging her gaze upward from his leg, over the expanse of tanned rock-hard abs and chest to his face.

His eyes were unreadable.

This was going to take courage.

"I…" She paused, drew in a deep breath, then shivered as the chilly breeze behind her ruffled her hair, skeining a long tress across her cheek and lips. She brushed it away, tucking it behind her ear, but before she could continue with her apology, Quinn reached out and caught her arm just above the elbow, tugging her forward.

"It's too damn cold to stand in this doorway," he explained when her gaze met his.

He pushed the door closed and eyed her, hands on hips. "You were saying?"

"I came to apologize," she said, deciding to meet the issue head-on.

His eyes went flat and his lips tightened, a muscle flexed along his jawline.

"I shouldn't have read your résumé—only town council members are supposed to have access to employee records. And I shouldn't have said you were addicted to danger," she hurried on, determined to get an apology out before he told her to leave.

"But you think it." His voice was grim, no emotion in the words.

"It's not personal. If I'd read anyone's résumé with a long list of life-threatening assignments in hostile places around the world, I would have concluded that the owner was a person who liked doing dangerous work."

"But it *is* personal. You do know me. My résumé isn't anonymous."

"True, your résumé isn't an unknown person's."

Abigail refused to retreat although he seemed to loom closer, big, dark, dangerous. "But your life experience is vastly different from mine. I was only trying to explain why we shouldn't get…involved. We have nothing in common beyond what seems to be mutual, overwhelming physical attraction."

"Overwhelming physical attraction." He repeated the words without inflection. "Tell me, Abby, just when did you read my résumé?"

"Why does it matter when I read it?" She frowned at him.

"Humor me. When?"

"I don't remember the exact date. Aunt Elizabeth left a copy on the dining room table, on top of a stack of papers she brought home from a town council meeting. The top page was your work history."

"So you knew about me before I came to Wolf Creek."

It wasn't a question, but Abigail answered anyway. "Yes."

"Women fall into two categories once they find out I was a sniper. Some run shrieking from the room and treat me like scum. Some are turned on and want to notch their bedpost by sleeping with a man who's killed." His eyes were gray ice. "Which category do you fall into, Abby?"

"Neither." Abigail was appalled.

"Yeah?" He prowled toward her.

Instinctively, she gave ground. She wasn't physically

afraid of him, but the sexual tension between them ratcheted higher with every moment.

Her shoulders bumped the door panel. He braced his forearms on the door beside her head, effectively pinning her against the wood although his body was still inches from hers. Heat poured off him, intensifying the natural scent she'd come to associate with only him. Her body yearned, melted.

Distracted by the physical, she struggled to remember what he'd said.

"No," she murmured, her voice a husky thread of sound. "I'm not."

"You're lying, Abby." He bent his head, his lips brushing her cheek as he whispered, "You're breathing too fast and your pulse is racing."

She tipped her head back, her gaze challenging his hooded, darkened stare. "I'm not turned on at the thought of you having done scary things."

"No?" His gaze flicked to her mouth, then back to her eyes. "Let's find out."

Abigail didn't have time to protest before his mouth took hers. His body lowered the few inches and settled over hers, his warm weight blanketing her much smaller frame.

His kiss was aggressively carnal and she had no defense against the wave of sheer need that swamped her. Her hands slipped around his neck, her fingers brushing his hair above his nape.

He lifted his head and looked down at her. Arousal

streaked color across the arch of his cheekbones, his mouth fuller, sensual.

"So tell me, is it lust or disgust you're feeling?" His voice was an octave deeper, silk over gravel.

"It's not disgust." She couldn't lie, despite knowing the truth was dangerous. Quinn was a threat to her heart and she'd just handed him the weapon to destroy her.

His eyes flared with heat, the hard lines of his face softening. His lashes lowered, hiding his eyes from her, and his mouth took hers once more.

But this kiss was different. Just as carnal but somehow softer, hotter, more seduction than lust.

Abigail abandoned herself to the sheer pleasure of being held in Quinn's arms, his mouth on hers, his hard body fitting against the soft curves of her own as if they'd been made expressly for each other.

She kissed him back.

The strident notes of a cell phone's ring sounded, the intrusion shattering the moment as surely as if Abigail had been ripped from Quinn's arms.

Abigail stiffened, suddenly aware of where she was and what she was doing. And who she was doing it with.

She forced her hands to uncurl from his nape and eased back, her palms flattening against his chest. The beat of his heart beneath her fingers was strong, fast and urged her to move closer. But somehow, she resisted.

"I have to go," she murmured.

His gray eyes were dark with arousal, lashes half

lowered over them. His arms tightened briefly, as if he meant to keep her with him, but then they loosened and his hands settled at her waist before he reached behind her and turned the knob.

She ducked under his arm and stepped outside.

"Have dinner with me tomorrow."

His words stopped her and she half turned to look back at him. "I shouldn't," she said softly.

"Why not? You have to eat, I have to eat…no reason we can't do it together."

She hesitated, torn between wanting to say yes and knowing she shouldn't spend more time with him because each moment in his company lured her closer.

"If I promise not to make a pass, will you go out with me?"

She searched his face and knew what it cost him to make the offer. "You'd do that?" she asked in disbelief.

"If that's the only way to get you to say yes," he said bluntly. "I'm not saying I *want* to keep my hands off you, I'm just saying I can, if you insist."

She studied him. He seemed sincere. In a rush, she threw caution to the winds. "All right. But I promised Tansy I'd read to her before she goes to sleep, so I'll need to be back by eight."

His slow grin melted her bones. "I'll pick you up at six."

"I'll be ready."

She turned and ran lightly down the steps. Two hours with Quinn in a public restaurant—no chance for giving in to temptation, right? She didn't look back as she crossed the lawn and entered the house, but she felt his gaze on her every step of the way.

Quinn knocked on the back door at exactly 6:00 p.m. Abigail stared, drinking him in. She hardly noticed when Buddy brushed past her and padded down the hall, on his way to the front parlor where Tansy, Elizabeth and Natasha were settled in with popcorn and a movie. Tansy had insisted the big dog stay at the house while Abigail and Quinn were out and had coaxed Quinn into agreeing to let Buddy spend the night for a sleepover.

"You're not thinking about canceling dinner with me, are you, Abby?" Quinn asked when she remained silent.

"No, of course not," she said. "But you promised you wouldn't…" She broke off before adding firmly, "I'm just trying to decide if I can trust you to keep your word."

"You can." He nodded solemnly to underline the words, but his mouth quirked, amusement lighting his gray eyes. "But I'm not sure I can trust you."

She sucked in a breath and felt her cheeks flush with heat. Damn the man. What was it about him that rattled her usual calm—especially when she knew he enjoyed shaking her composure and did it on purpose?

"Just so you know," he said, leaning forward to murmur in her ear, "if you change your mind, I wouldn't be upset if you decided you can't keep your hands off me tonight." His lips curved with amusement, his eyes heating.

"I think I can control myself," she said dryly.

"Too bad," he drawled, stepping aside to wave her ahead of him. "Good night, ladies," he called down the hall as Abigail moved past him and outside.

"'Night, Quinn," the aunts and Tansy chorused from the front parlor. Buddy didn't so much as utter a woof and Quinn suspected he was curled up at Tansy's feet, probably trying to coax her into giving him a handful of her popcorn.

Quinn pulled the door closed behind him and joined Abigail to walk across the back lawn to his truck. Conversation was desultory as they drove downtown, as if each were purposely focusing on noncontroversial topics. They talked about the weather—both agreed it was chilly but not terribly so, considering it was late September. They talked about how her great-aunts were coping with a lively four-year-old in the house—both agreed Elizabeth and Natasha appeared to be energized by Tansy.

Fortunately, they parked and walked into the restaurant before they ran out of polite, innocuous conversation.

They paused just inside the tiled entry, glancing around the busy room, and a young woman carrying menus approached them.

"Hello, Abigail." She looked at Quinn, then lifted a brow at Abigail. Her eyes sparkled with curiosity. "Table for two?"

"Yes, please, Rebecca," Abigail murmured, returning the smile and pretending to ignore the question in

Rebecca's eyes. The young woman was the daughter of the restaurant's manager; Abigail saw her at least once a week but rarely with a man in tow.

Fortunately, Rebecca managed to contain her curiosity and left them at their table with menus and a promise to send their waiter over.

Quinn opened his menu and scanned the pages quickly, then glanced up at her. "You must eat here often," he commented, indicating her closed menu with a wave of his hand. "What do you recommend?"

"The New York steak is always good and if you like seafood, I can recommend the trout."

"Steak for me." He snapped his menu closed and shifted it to the edge of the table. "You?" He lifted an eyebrow in query.

"Steak and salad." She waited until the approaching waiter had taken their orders and left them with glasses of ice water. "I understand you're from Seattle. I'm surprised you didn't order the fish."

"Seattle has some of the best seafood in the world," he agreed. "And salmon grilled on cedar plank is a favorite of mine—but I'm originally from the Southwest. Steak is high on my favorite food list."

"That's good news for the locals," she said with a laugh. "Ranchers around Wolf Creek tend to get annoyed when visitors turn up their noses at beef."

"I can see why." He smiled at her, sun lines crinkling at the corners of his eyes.

"What part of the Southwest are you from?" Abigail asked, curious.

"Texas, originally, followed by New Mexico. But I left there when I was sixteen."

"A city in Texas and New Mexico? Or ranch country?"

"Ranch country." He sipped his water, his gray eyes watching her over the glass rim. "I worked as a cowhand before I enlisted in the marines."

Abigail felt her eyes go round. "Maybe that's why you three look so much alike," she murmured aloud.

"We three?" He lifted a brow in question. "What three?"

"You, Zach Kerrigan and Chase McCloud." Abigail waved a hand dismissively. "I happened to see the three of you standing together in the banquet room last week and it struck me that there seemed to be a resemblance."

His eyes narrowed and for a fleeting moment, she thought she saw a flash of darkness there, but then Quinn smiled and he was once again the affable, handsome charmer.

"Interesting."

"You've all worked on ranches and of course, there's also the fact that each of you was in the military." She frowned, considering. "I don't believe Zach has been an investigator, but both you and Chase work with Colter Investigations out of Seattle, don't you?" She met his gaze and spread her hands in a shrug. "I just thought it was interesting that your lives seemed to parallel each other."

The waitress arrived with their dinner, deftly sliding Abigail's onto the white-cloth-covered table before her.

"Evidently." Quinn leaned back to allow the waitress to place a steaming plate in front of him.

Conversation turned to generalities about her work at the library, Quinn listening with obvious interest as she told him anecdotes about some of the more interesting characters. Their waitress cleared their plates and brought them after-dinner coffee and Abigail realized the time had flown.

Quinn leaned back in his chair, seemingly relaxed and mellow with good food. "So, tell me about your town. You've lived here…how long?"

"Since birth." Abigail couldn't suppress a smile at the swift disbelief that flashed across his features. "Probably seems strange to someone who's apparently been footloose for so long but yes, I've lived in Wolf Creek all my life. Except for the few years in college," she amended.

"You like this town that much?"

She nodded, her gaze moving across the room before returning to meet his. "Yes." She smiled. "I lived in Los Angeles for five years while I studied for my degree at UCLA and I enjoyed the city—beautiful beaches, fun at Disneyland, beautiful people…" Her voice trailed off and for a moment, she was distracted by the absence of the expected twist of pain that usually accompanied the memories of California, college and Manny. "But..." she continued, her mouth losing its faintly sad, downward curve, "I'm happiest here." She shrugged. "I guess I'm a small-town girl at heart." She lifted her cup and sipped, eyeing him calmly over the rim.

"Nothing wrong with knowing where you belong," Quinn agreed.

"What about you?" Abigail asked. "Where do you belong—what place means home to you?"

He shrugged. "I suppose it's Seattle, for now. That's my mailing address and it's where my apartment is—where I store my hiking gear. But I'm not there often," he added.

"So, no home, really, at least not in the usual sense of the word."

"The apartment is as close to a home as I'm likely to get." He grinned when she frowned and shook her head. "I suppose I'm a wanderer—home and permanence aren't on my radar."

"Well, that's just crazy. Everybody belongs some-where."

"Evidently not." Quinn chuckled, amused at the stubborn, militant lift of her chin. "I'm guessing we're on opposite sides of the fence on this one, Abby. We'll just have to agree to disagree."

"I'm not sure I..." she began, glancing past his shoulder, distracted by the sound of raised voices. "Oh, no," she murmured with frustration.

Quinn registered the annoyed resignation in her voice

and noted the faint frown veeing her brows. Following her gaze, he glanced over his shoulder.

A tall, lean man walked toward them, waving off the hostess.

"Tell the waitress I want a steak with all the trimmings. I'll be there as soon as I say hello to Abigail. And bring me a whiskey and water."

The hostess gave him a brief nod. Before she turned away, Quinn saw the wry look of apology she sent Abigail.

"I take it he's a friend of yours?" he asked.

Abby's quick shake of her head answered his question, but before she could speak, the man reached their table.

"Evening, Abigail," he said.

"Hello, Roger." Abigail's reply was cool but friendly. "How are you?"

"Fine—and you?" Roger inquired.

"I'm fine, as well. How's your mother?"

"She's in Denver at the moment on a shopping trip."

"Ah." Abigail's lips quirked in a wry smile, but she didn't elaborate. Her gaze met Quinn's and she lifted a brow in inquiry. "Have you met Roger Hansen, Quinn? His law office is just off Main Street on Spruce Avenue."

"No, I haven't." Quinn gave the man a smile that was all teeth, caught off guard by a surge of territorial possessiveness that flared to life. Hansen had a distinctly proprietorial air toward Abigail and it annoyed the hell out of Quinn. "I'm filling in until Wolf Creek hires a permanent replacement for sheriff."

"Nice to meet you." Roger's reply was brusque and just shy of rude, his smile not reaching his eyes. "I was out of town and just returned, unfortunately too late to attend the welcoming party. I'm sure you probably met most of the town's business owners."

"I did," Quinn agreed with a nod. "Nice group of folks."

Roger's handsome face creased in a stiff, brief smile. "Yes, they are." He turned back to Abigail. "We need to get together to talk about the library fundraiser. Maybe over dinner this week?"

"I'll check my calendar and get back to you," she responded. Quinn didn't miss what seemed to be a purposefully vague, noncommittal response and clearly, neither did Roger, who frowned.

"I'll call you," he said firmly.

"Mr. Hansen?" The hostess approached. "Your dinner is being served. If you'll follow me to your table?"

"Give my best to your mother," Abigail said.

"I'll do that." He nodded goodbye and left.

Quinn's gaze followed him across the room to a table for one.

"A frustrated suitor?" he asked Abigail lazily.

"I doubt it," she answered, clearly amused. "I'm more inclined to think he sees me as his way into the inner circle of local society. He's wrong, of course," she added. "Wolf Creek doesn't really have levels of society—we're pretty democratically inclined. Which I've told him on several occasions, in every way I know how, but he just won't accept it. Roger has political aspirations and sees Wolf Creek as a stepping stone to bigger and better things."

"If he wants a political career, why didn't he open a law practice in Helena?"

"An office in the state capital seems the most logical choice to me, too," she agreed. "The only possible reason I can see for him choosing Wolf Creek is that the McCloud family lives here. They're politically connected and powerful, with a lot of influence in the state legislature. Beyond that—" she shook her head "—I confess his reasoning baffles me."

"Maybe his interest isn't connected to politics."

"What do you mean?"

"You're a beautiful woman, Abby. A man would be interested in you for that alone."

She stared at him for a long moment, clearly speechless. Then she laughed, a low throaty chuckle that had Quinn's body clenching at the sound.

"You're such a charmer, Quinn McCloud," she said at last, mirth still curving her lips and sparkling in the depths of blue eyes. "I bet you don't even know you're doing it, do you?"

"Doing what?" he said, perplexed.

"Blowing smoke." She leaned forward, her silky hair falling forward, the ends curling just above the tips of her breasts. "It's as natural to you as breathing."

Quinn shook his head, narrowed his eyes over her smiling face. "Why do you find it so hard to believe I'm sincere?"

"Because I've known a couple of men just like you," she told him breezily. "My father, bless his dearly departed heart, could charm the birds out of the trees. Women loved him—followed him around as if he were the Pied Piper himself."

"And he broke their hearts?" Quinn hazarded.

"No, goodness no." Abigail shook her head. "He loved them right back. All of them. Aunt Elizabeth told me Daddy fell in love every Friday night down at the saloon and had his heart broken when he woke up every Monday morning. He was totally sincere, poor man."

"And you think I'm the same?" Quinn knew he sounded offended. *Hell,* he thought, *I* am *offended.*

"Don't take it the wrong way," she said hastily. "I didn't mean to insult you. I loved Daddy—everyone did. It's just that after knowing him, it's pretty much impossible for me to believe any comments from a man as charming and handsome as him."

"You think I'm charming and handsome?" Quinn felt ridiculously pleased, opting to skip her implication that she apparently thought she couldn't believe anything he said.

Abigail glanced down, her lashes lowering to shield her eyes, then looked back up at him, the thick fringe concealing her thoughts. "I'm sure you know just how charming you are. And I'm only telling you this to let you know that flattery won't work on me. I may be seriously tempted but I won't give in."

"Well, I'll be damned," Quinn said mildly. "You're a rare woman, Abby Foster."

"Thank you. I think," she added, eyeing him. She glanced at her watch and frowned. "It's getting late. I promised Tansy I'd be home in time to read to her before she falls asleep."

"Lucky Tansy." He leaned forward, the candlelight flickering over his face. "If you ever feel like tucking me in, let me know."

And just that quickly, Abigail was awash in heat. She knew her face must have flushed with color because Quinn grinned, amusement—and something sultrier—in his eyes, and lifted a hand to summon their waitress. Moments later, they left the restaurant and headed for home.

Quinn turned off the street and drove down the alley behind her house, the pickup truck's tires crunching over gravel when he parked next to the garage.

He'd forgotten to turn on the apartment's outside entry light. When he switched off the key, the sudden darkness enclosed the truck cab in intimacy.

True to his word, however, Quinn didn't take advantage. Instead, he opened the driver's door and stepped out, rounding the hood of the truck.

Abigail unlatched her seat belt and slipped it free, bending to collect her purse from the floor at her feet.

Before she could push the door open, however, Quinn was there, holding it wide.

He held out his hand. She gave fleeting thought to ignoring it before deciding to accept the polite gesture.

She wondered about the wisdom of her decision when his hand closed around hers. Warm, hard, faintly rough with calluses, his hand enfolding hers sent a wave of warmth and an unexpected feeling of being cherished and protected washing over her.

Startled, she met his gaze. But instead of the knowing male satisfaction she expected to find there, she caught a flash of surprise and some darker emotion before she dropped her gaze and stepped out of the truck.

He freed her the moment she stood on the ground, the vehicle's door closing with a quiet thunk, leaving them in the night's dimness.

"Does Buddy stay in the apartment while you're at work?" she asked as she turned to cross the lawn, aware of his broad-shouldered body moving beside her.

"No, I take him to the office with me most mornings," Quinn said. "Karl and Sarah think he's great. I'm not sure they'd mind if I didn't show up for work, but they'd definitely miss Buddy if he wasn't there."

They reached the back porch and climbed the steps, Quinn pushing the door open and following her inside. Abigail fit her key into the inner door to the kitchen and twisted the dead bolt free before turning to look up at him.

"I had a lovely time tonight, Quinn," she murmured. "Thank you for dinner."

"You're welcome. I had a good time, too." His fingers brushed against her cheek, tucking a strand of hair behind her ear. His hand was warm, the air was cold. "I promised I wouldn't make a pass at you." The pad of his thumb stroked over her cheek. "But I'd really like to kiss you good-night, Abby."

The faint light from the streetlamp outside threw shadows over his face, highlighting the hard thrust of his cheekbones and making dark pools of his eyes.

"I'd like that," she said, already yearning.

A faint smile curved the hard line of his mouth before he cupped her face in his hands and bent his head. His lips were warm and for long, breath-stealing moments they covered hers. When at last he lifted his head, Abigail's heart was pounding, her head swimming.

"Good night," his deep voice rasped, the murmur dark as the night outside. He reached behind her and pushed the door inward, waiting until she stepped inside the kitchen before pulling the door shut, closing her away.

Abigail stood without moving, staring at the door panels without seeing them. It wasn't until she heard the sharp bark as Buddy raced down the stairs from Tansy's room that she realized she'd been standing, staring in bemusement at the door, for long moments.

She turned and left the kitchen, shedding her coat and gloves as she climbed the stairs. The sound of giggles, splashing and Natasha's voice from the upstairs bathroom told her Tansy was having her bath.

Abigail took a precious few moments to hang up her coat in her bedroom and compose herself before joining the two. It wasn't until a few hours later that she went to bed—and dreamed about Quinn.

Chapter Eight

Quinn and Buddy resumed their habit of walking across the backyard and joining Abigail in the kitchen for coffee before heading to the sheriff's office each morning. Sometimes Tansy was there, sometimes not. Usually, the great-aunts were ensconced in the living room, having their morning tea or coffee and catching up on the latest news on cable TV.

One Saturday morning, Quinn walked to work with Abigail, who'd left home early in order to let Tansy play in the park with the neighborhood children.

"You're good with kids," Quinn commented, watching Tansy race away across the grass to rejoin the other children at the swing sets.

"I like children," she responded.

She sat in profile to him, an indulgent smile curving her mouth, her gaze on the group of chattering little girls.

"Ever think about getting married and having a few?" He brushed his fingertips beneath the thick fall of her hair and over the soft skin of her nape.

She turned her head to glance sideways at him through half-lowered lashes. The move sent her hair sliding silkily over his hand and wrist. "Sometimes," she said. Her blue eyes darkened a shade. "I was married once," she said softly.

Quinn's fingers stilled on her soft, warm skin as an unexpected surge of possessiveness washed over him. "What happened?" he managed to ask.

"He was killed."

Swift sympathy eased the tension from his frame. "I'm sorry, honey." He gently tugged and she let him pull her closer, not protesting when he pressed his lips to the baby-soft skin at her temple. His hand cupped her nape. "That's rough. No one in town mentioned to me that you'd been married."

"No one in Wolf Creek knows," she said quietly. "Except my aunts."

He tipped his head back and looked down at her, searching her eyes. "Why not?"

"We eloped to Vegas and got married when we were both students at UCLA." Her gaze left his and she looked down at her hands, clasped tightly together in her lap. "Manny was killed in a street race six months after the wedding. I stayed on in Los Angeles until I graduated from college."

"And then you came home to Wolf Creek." It wasn't a question. Quinn guessed she'd come home to heal in the quiet safety of this small town.

"That's right." She looked up at him. "I know my friends and neighbors would have been supportive but I wasn't ready to deal with well-meaning conversations. I always planned to tell folks at some point but…" She shrugged. "By the time I felt ready to cope with being a widow, the opportunity to broach the subject seemed to have passed. So I didn't tell anyone."

"Is that why you don't date?" He wondered if she still hadn't recovered from losing a husband while so young.

"Partly," she admitted. "And if I'm being completely honest, I suppose I'm not eager to get involved again."

"Why not?"

"Because I seem to be attracted to men who like to live dangerously. My husband loved to race but he chose to do it illegally on city streets in Los Angeles. The fact that he was breaking the law only seemed to make it more appealing. And now—" She met his gaze, her eyes troubled "—there's you."

"I don't indulge in illegal racing," he told her gently.

"No," she agreed. "Thank goodness. But your occupation isn't the safest. You're in law enforcement and carry a gun. That's not a good indicator that nothing will ever happen to you."

"Maybe not, but statistics show that law enforcement isn't the most dangerous job in the U.S. In fact," he added, "it's not even in the top ten."

"Really?" she said skeptically. "What is?"

"Number one is loggers, second is fisherman, third is pilots. I don't remember numbers four through ten, but trust me," he told her. "Being a cop of any kind isn't in the top ten."

"Hmm." Her mouth curved in a slow smile. "So perhaps I should just make sure I don't fall in love with a logger, fisherman or pilot."

He shrugged. "Sounds like a good plan. Were any of them on your list for possible fathers of those kids you'd like to have?"

"No," she murmured, her lashes lowered as her gaze traced his face.

"Good." Quinn's voice was deeper, rougher. "I'll have to convince you to move 'sheriff' to the top of that list."

Her eyes widened and her gaze flew to meet his.

Quinn easily read her wariness. Reluctantly, he decided she wasn't ready to talk about the sexual tension that hummed between them.

"Of course, first I have to convince you to go out with me," he drawled with a lazy grin.

The easing comment diffused the tension and Abigail visibly relaxed.

"I'm guessing you say that to all the girls," she shot back.

"Why, Miss Abby," he said with pretend shock. "Are you suggesting I'm not sincere?"

Amusement sparkled in her blue eyes. "That's a definite 'yes.'" She glanced at her watch and her eyes widened. "Look at the time. I'll be late for work!" She jumped to her feet, calling to Tansy.

Quinn rose lazily to join her, amused by her quick return to the efficient, independent career-woman persona that he now knew was only one of the many sides of Abigail Foster.

Abigail had yet to ask for more than kisses and Quinn was still managing to keep from tossing her over his shoulder and heading for his apartment and bedroom.

But it had been a near thing on several occasions, he reflected late one afternoon as he sat in his office, a reminiscent smile curving his lips.

The intercom buzzed, breaking into his thoughts, and he leaned forward to switch it on.

"Sheriff, you have a visitor—it's Chase McCloud."

"Send him in, Sarah." Quinn flipped the intercom off and stood just as the office door opened.

"Hey, Chase, come on in." Quinn waved him toward a chair facing the desk. "What brings you here?"

"Just stopped to say hello." The rancher dropped into the wooden chair, crossing one ankle over the other knee and shoving his Stetson back off his brow. "I told Ren I'd keep track of you."

"Yeah, right," Quinn said dryly. He leaned back in his chair and propped his crossed ankles on the corner of the desk. "More likely Ren told you to harass me."

Chase grinned, blue eyes twinkling. "Now that you mention it, the word 'harass' did come up."

"Somehow, I'm not surprised."

"Anything new on the burglary at the Madsen Ranch?"

"Not much. Karl's been complaining he's reached a dead end. Have you heard any rumors floating around about kids being involved?"

"Not a thing." Chase shook his head. "But it might have been kids with a few beers and the urge to break the law."

"Maybe. But I've been going over Sheriff Adam's file of ongoing cases within a hundred-mile radius and there's a pattern. No burglaries prior to this one in this county, but in states bordering us, there's been a rash of them."

"Really?" Chase sat forward, his gaze sharpening. "Tell me."

Quinn dropped his feet to the floor and stood, crossing to the huge map of Montana, the Dakotas to the east, Wyoming to the south and Idaho to the west.

"I marked the reports of burglaries with red push pins." He pointed at the map.

Chase joined him, hands on hips, as he followed Quinn's pointing finger.

"You can see the pattern," Quinn said. "There's been

a rash of burglaries through the Dakotas, and south of us in Wyoming. Not a lot in Idaho. I've requested but haven't received reports from states farther east, but I wouldn't be surprised if they had an increase in break-ins a month or more ago."

Chase stared at the map, eyes narrowing. "So what are you thinking?"

"Looks like an organized theft ring." Quinn pointed to the march of red pins across the map. "Maybe they've got locals involved, maybe not. If they don't, it'll be harder to predict where they'll hit next. But if you look at the number of times some counties across the state line from us in North Dakota were hit, I'd guess Wolf Creek is in for a rough few weeks. And soon."

Chase's mouth set in a grim line. He stepped closer, the better to read the dates on the North Dakota burglaries. "Some of the dates are weeks apart."

"If you look at the South Dakota and Wyoming dates, you'll see why."

Chase's gaze flicked to the dates written in small letters next to the red pins. "I'll be damned. What do the interstate law enforcement people say about this?"

"Nothing."

Chase's head snapped around. "Nothing?"

Quinn shook his head. "Not a damn thing. If I didn't know better, I'd think they haven't figured it out yet."

"Seems pretty clear to me."

"Yeah, that's what I think."

"So what do you suppose is going on?"

Quinn eyed the big map. "There are two possibilities. Either all the cops in a six-state radius are blind, or there's a sting going on and law enforcement is locked down."

"Was there anything in Sheriff Adams's files about it?"

"Not that I can find."

"What did the state guys say?"

"I have a call in to them. They haven't called back. I'll give them another call tomorrow morning if I don't hear before."

"My dad has a lot of connections in the state capital. Want me to ask him to make a few calls, see if he can learn anything?"

Quinn shook his head. "I don't want to take this outside the law enforcement community—at least, not yet. If there's an agent undercover, I don't want to risk exposing him."

"All right, but the offer stands if you decide you need it."

"Thanks."

As Quinn and Chase were saying goodbye, across the street in the library, Tansy was keeping Abigail company.

The children's area of the library was like a second home to Abigail. She'd spent countless hours as a child sitting in one of the tiny slotted chairs that circled the matching oak table, her fingers eagerly turning pages until she'd looked through each and every book in the section. She could see herself in her mind's eye even now, so small, but with such a ferocious appetite for the adventures that only books could provide.

Tansy flipped from her tummy onto her back, her hair fanning out on the colorful area rug where she lay, a hardback copy of *Where the Wild Things Are* open and propped on her bent knees. The little girl had grown more comfortable with Abigail and her aunts over the last few days, her need for a connection clearly outweighing everything else. Abigail watched her as she read, her face filling with delight as Max's journey trundled along in the book. The dimming light of the afternoon sun arrowed through the tall window and gleamed off streaks of gold in Tansy's brown hair, making it shimmer against the deep reds and blues of the carpet.

"Tansy," Abigail said softly.

The little girl looked up at Abigail and lowered the book to the floor beside her. "Hmm?"

"You're an awfully good reader for your age," Abigail said nonchalantly, looking up from the paperwork she'd been leafing through.

"My daddy was, too," Tansy began, clearly pleased with the comment. "He says reading is very important and that I should practice every day."

Abigail smiled gently at the child, trying not to show her interest. "Did he learn to read from Elizabeth?"

"I dunno," Tansy began, a puzzled frown pulling the soft wings of her eyebrows closer together. "But he did spend lots and lots of time here. Oh—and Miss Elizabeth read to him while he was here, so I guess you could say that she helped."

Abigail stacked the papers and put them back into their manila file folder. "I think you're right and Elizabeth definitely helped your daddy become good at reading." She picked up her pen and the folder. "Did your daddy have a favorite book?"

Tansy's brows furrowed as she thought. "Bruno and somebody, I think."

"*Bruno and Biggs?*" Abigail asked, the series of books about a boy and his crime-solving canine coming instantly to mind. Her encyclopedic brain for all things books told her that the series had only been around since the early seventies, which meant Tansy's father couldn't be much older then herself.

"That's it!" Tansy said gleefully, just as the open book on her knee fell, crumpling several pages. "Oh, no."

Abigail stood, the folder and pen in her hand. She held out the other for Tansy and gestured for the girl to take it. "It's all right, Tansy. You're not in trouble."

The little girl took Abigail's hand and allowed herself to be pulled up. "Are you sure?"

"Very sure," Abigail said reassuringly, squeezing the little girl's tiny hand in hers. "But you know who will be in trouble if these books aren't put away?" she asked, a mock look of horror on her face as she pointed to the large stack of books on the table.

Tansy giggled and pointed at Abigail.

"That's right. Now let's get these put away so we can head home. Tonight is spaghetti night in the Foster household and I don't know about you, but I hate cold spaghetti!"

"Me, too!" Tansy replied, then stuck out her tongue and made a gagging sound.

The two quietly giggled, then set to work, Abigail showing Tansy how to read the numbers on the book's spine, then guiding her to the proper shelves.

So her father clearly spent time in Wolf Creek when he was a child, and he couldn't be more than ten years older than herself, Abigail thought as she stole a glance at Tansy, the little girl's concentration on the task at hand charming. She'd have to talk to Elizabeth right away. Maybe the information would jog her aunt's memory about the identity of Tansy's father.

And then she'd have to see Quinn. Abigail didn't know if it was the possible clue in the information or the impending meeting that made her heart skip a beat, and she wasn't entirely sure that she wanted to find out. She called his office and left a message to contact her.

Unfortunately for Abigail, Quinn didn't come home at the usual time and she went to bed without seeing him, disappointed and wondering where he was and if he was safe.

The rattle of what sounded like hail against her windowpane woke Abigail from a vivid dream of making love with Quinn. Disoriented, she glanced at the bedside clock and it took a moment for her to realize it read 12:30 a.m. She tossed back the covers and hurried across the room to close the window, pausing to frown at the sky where dark clouds partially obscured the full moon.

It's not storming, she thought, confused.

Something pattered against the glass pane again. Startled, she looked down at the yard below.

Quinn stood on the lawn, his face turned up to her. He beckoned, lips moving, and she slid the window higher so she could hear him.

"Come down," he said, his voice throttled to a deep whisper.

"It's the middle of the night," she whispered back, hoping the sound wouldn't wake her aunts.

"You left a message. Come down and tell me what you wanted."

She was tempted, so very tempted. Her pulse was still pounding faster than normal from the dream.

Why not? she thought recklessly. "I'll be right down," she called softly.

Feeling like a teenager sneaking out of the house for a forbidden date, Abigail stripped out of her pajamas and pulled on her jeans. She skipped a bra and tugged a sweater over her head, shoved her bare feet into her slippers, and headed quietly downstairs, slipping her arms into her jacket as she went.

The moment she opened the back door and stepped outside, she shivered.

"Brrrr, it's cold out here," she told him, hugging her arms around her. The moonlight gleamed on his black hair and threw shadows over his face. When he grinned at her, his teeth flashed white. She was instantly, help-lessly enthralled.

"Sorry, I've been outside for a while and stopped noticing the temp." He stepped closer, wrapped his arm around her shoulders and hustled her with him across the lawn. "Let's get you inside where it's warm."

She had to hurry to keep up with his longer strides but didn't protest. He slowed when they reached the steps leading to the garage apartment, releasing her shoulder to take her hand as they climbed. He unlocked the door and pulled her inside.

"Lots warmer in here," he told her. He leaned past her to flip the lamp switch, his chest pressing against her breasts as he did so. The lamp beside the sofa flicked on, illuminating the room with soft light, casting shad-ows into the corners.

Abigail caught her breath when his body touched hers. She instinctively shifted back from the electric contact and her shoulders bumped the door panel. Quinn went still, his gaze sharpening as he stared down at her.

"Abby?" he murmured, his voice deeper, husky.

She couldn't reply. Being alone with him in the shadowed room, with the memory of the heated dream still vivid in her mind, was suddenly too intimate and far, far too dangerous. She knew she needed to find her voice and tell him she had to leave.

Quinn didn't give her time to act.

His gray eyes darkened to nearly black and he closed the small distance between them until only inches separated them. He planted the palms of both hands on the wooden door, effectively caging her. The he leaned forward and covered her mouth with his.

The kiss wasn't the heated assault she'd expected. His lips softly coaxed her to relax, seducing the heat already burning in her body and making it burst into flames. Abigail slid her arms around his neck and tugged him closer until the hard planes of his body were molded to hers. She nearly groaned when he obeyed, his arms wrapping around her waist and lifting her onto her toes as the kiss turned carnal, demanding.

Quinn's hands cupped her bottom and lifted her.

"Put your legs around my waist, honey," he muttered, his voice a deep growl.

She complied, the move pressed the V of her legs against his zipper and Abby moved closer, shifting against him.

Quinn growled a curse and strode down the hall. He set her on her feet next to the bed and unceremoniously stripped her jacket off, shrugging off his own. They dropped unnoticed to the floor and he caught the hem of her sweater.

"Wait." Her hand closed on his and he tensed. Nearly dizzy with desire, Abigail searched his eyes and struggled for sanity. "Should we be doing this?"

The dim light from the hall let her read the heat and conviction in his eyes.

"Oh, yeah." His mouth curled in a half grin, his bottom lip fuller, sensual. "We should have done this days ago."

He brushed her mouth with his, gently, wooing her, sending her fears flying.

"But if you don't want to, tell me now," he murmured against her throat. "Because in about two seconds, I'm gonna have a hard time stopping."

"Don't stop," she breathed and cupped her hands against his face, drawing his mouth back to hers.

The speed with which he stripped the rest of their clothes off left her gasping. He pulled a small square packet from his jeans, ripped it open with his teeth and donned protection. Then he laid her on the bed, following her down and blanketing her with heady, warm weight.

He nudged her knees apart and Abigail struggled to accommodate him before he slid home. She groaned with relief before Quinn started moving and sent her soaring.

The second time they made love was slower and Quinn took his time, tormenting her with caresses and kisses until she begged him to stop teasing and take her.

After the third time, they lay in bed, talking between kisses, the edge of their hunger blunted but not gone.

"I can't believe I'm the only one with secrets,"

Abby told him. She rested her folded arms on his bare chest and eyed him. "Come on, McCloud, 'fess up. What skeletons are rattling their bones in your closet?" she teased.

"None." He laughed when she moved and swatted his bicep, lifting just enough to give him a glimpse of the bare curves of her breasts. He smoothed his palms down her back and cupped her bottom, pressing her closer.

"Don't distract me." She narrowed her eyes at him despite a shiver that shifted her against him. "I told you my secret—that I was married and widowed. In the interests of fair play, you have to tell me something— something no one else knows about you. And it has to be personal."

"Personal?" He could have told her he didn't confide in the women that moved through his life. But she wasn't just another woman. She was Abby, and every- thing about knowing her was different from everyone else in his past. He eyed her and made a decision. "First you have to swear you won't tell anyone."

She waved a hand dismissively. "That goes without saying."

He nodded. "I'm John McCloud's nephew."

Her eyes widened. It was a full second before she could respond. "Wow." A frown knit her brows. "But I asked you when we met if you were related to Chase McCloud and you said no."

"I said I first met Chase McCloud when I went to

work for Ren at the agency," Quinn corrected her. "I never lied to you. I just didn't tell you the whole truth."

Abby looked as if she wanted to argue the point but then shrugged as if to say she had more interesting questions. "Does Chase know?"

"No."

"Why not?" She frowned. "How could he not know?"

"Because my father—John McCloud's brother—never married my mother. In fact, he died before I was born.

"I vaguely remember my great-aunts talking about John McCloud's brother. Wasn't he killed at a rodeo?"

"Yeah, that's what I understand. He died in Mexico." Quinn scanned her expectant, intrigued expression and sighed. Clearly, she wanted the details. "My mother was from a small town in Texas. She met Sean McCloud at a local rodeo and joined him on the road. They were in Mexico when he was killed in the arena and she returned to Texas. She took a job waitressing in a bar and married the owner when I was around two years old. He adopted me but we never got along. I left home at sixteen, and when I turned eighteen, I had the adoption records opened. Learned my real father's name was McCloud, and had my name changed before I joined the army. That's about it."

She blinked her eyes at the rapid-fire explanation. "Again, wow. That's quite a story." She thought a moment. "But that doesn't' explain why John McCloud doesn't know you're his nephew. Haven't you told him?"

"No. And I don't plan to."

"Why not?" Her surprise was written on her face and in her puzzled voice.

"Because everything I know about families tells me they're way more trouble than they're worth," he said bluntly. "Starting with my mother and stepfather."

Abigail was silent for a long moment. "I'm sorry, Quinn," she said, soft regret coloring her voice. "I sometimes forget that not everyone's relatives are as great as mine." She leaned forward and kissed him, her lips lingering before she lifted her head. "But I think you should tell John and Margaret McCloud and their sons. They really are good people. I've never heard my aunts or Walt—or anyone else whose opinion I respect—utter a bad word about them.

"They seem to be decent folks," he agreed. "But no outsider ever knows what goes on behind closed doors— my stepfather's friends thought he was a great guy."

She stiffened, her soft curves going taut against his. "Did he hurt you?" she demanded fiercely.

"What? No," he reassured her. Her first instinct was clearly to do damage to anyone who harmed him, and he grinned, delighted. "You look like you're ready to grab a gun and go looking for him."

"I would, if he's been mean to you," she said firmly.

He instantly decided never to tell her about the beatings his stepfather had administered with a belt. Quinn had left his parents' home in Texas and never looked back. He wasn't a guy with unresolved issues about the sorry excuse of a man his mother had married.

"Don't worry about it, Abby." He nuzzled the soft skin of her throat just beneath her chin. "I sure as hell don't."

Her hands gripped his biceps and her fingers curled, flexing. He heard the swift intake of her breath as his mouth moved lower to capture the tip of her breast.

"Quinn."

The single, breathy sound of his name on her lips told him all he needed to know. She wanted him. He rolled, tucking her beneath him, he wanted her, too. He refused to think about the edge of need beneath the sheer lust that drove him to claim her.

Quinn walked into the café just down the street from the sheriff's office and paused, scanning the room. At 6:30 a.m., the restaurant was doing a thriving business with a breakfast crowd that filled most of the seats. The chatter of conversations joined the clink of glassware and cutlery, raising the noise level until he could barely hear the country-western song playing on the radio behind the counter. The smell of fresh coffee brewing and bacon frying filled the air, teasing his senses, and made him realize just how hungry he was. He'd been called out to assist with a two-car crash involving tourists late the prior afternoon and just as he was getting ready to head for home around 9:00 p.m., Karl had radioed. The deputy wanted his input at the scene of a suspicious fire on a ranch located near the far southern border of the county. They'd returned to the office and the inevitable paperwork just before 5:00 a.m. Which meant he hadn't slept in twenty-four hours and hadn't eaten for more than twelve.

"Hey, Quinn."

He scanned the room and found Chase and John McCloud beckoning to him from a booth toward the back. He lifted a hand in reply and wound his way around the tables to reach them.

"Join us," John said.

"Thanks." Quinn shrugged out of his jacket and hung it on the hook on the booth before sliding in beside Chase. "This place is packed."

"They're always busy for breakfast," Chase agreed. "Great food."

"Good news, since I'm starved," Quinn said.

John grinned but before he could reply, a waitress stopped, poured coffee for Quinn without asking, set the glass coffeepot down and poised her pencil over her pad. "What'll it be?"

The moment she jotted down their orders, she quickly topped off their mugs and bustled off.

"That's why we like coming here," Chase commented with a grin. "Very little hassle, fast food."

"Sounds good to me," Quinn sipped his coffee and thanked the gods it was hot and strong. His eyes felt as if there were sand in them.

"You're out early," Chase said, his eyes shrewd.

"I've been out all night," Quinn answered, rubbing his eyes with thumb and forefinger. The action didn't seem to help the gritty feeling.

"What's going on?" John's question was mild, but the sharp interest in his dark blue eyes was anything but.

"Somebody broke into the Harris place south of town," Quinn replied.

"They're south, almost to the county line," Chase put in. "Was anybody home?"

"No." Quinn shook his head. "The family was in Denver, got home around nine."

"I swear," John said with disgust. "Whoever's pulling these robberies must be local—they only hit when the owners are gone for a few days. We're damned lucky they didn't rob our place when Margaret and I were away. I suppose they probably would have if we didn't have hired hands and a bunkhouse close to the main house. Whoever it is must be local. How else could they keep tabs on which ranchers were away from home unless they lived around here?"

"I wouldn't argue with your logic, John." Quinn emptied his coffee mug and looked around for the waitress. He caught her eye, lifted his mug and she nodded.

Seconds later, she appeared with three plates of food balanced on her arms and more coffee.

The three men concentrated on their breakfast, conversation brief.

"What are you two doing in town this early?" Quinn asked as they emptied their plates and sat back.

"We're on our way to Billings." Chase nodded at John. "Dad wants to talk to a rodeo contractor about a young bull he thinks might be a good prospect for the arena."

"I didn't know you raised rodeo stock," Quinn said.

"McClouds have been connected to the rodeo for over eighty years." John pointed at the wall beside them where a collection of black-and-white photos, framed in plain black, hung. "That's my brother Sean."

Quinn's grip on his mug twitched, spilling a few drops of coffee, and he hoped to hell neither John nor Chase noticed his reaction. He leaned forward, the better to see the photos. He'd found a couple of pictures of Sean McCloud on an Internet rodeo fan site, but they hadn't been close-ups.

Most of the framed photos on the wall here were long shots, too, and taken in a dusty arena, the center of the picture a bucking horse with a man on his back. One of the photos was a group of men and Quinn recognized a much younger John, his arm over the shoulders of a laughing man who looked a lot like him.

Despite never having seen a close-up, Quinn knew the man with John was probably Sean, which made the guy his biological father. But he felt nothing—there was no instant gut recognition or connection.

"He was a rodeo rider?" he asked, his voice revealing only mild curiosity.

"Yeah, ever since he was a kid—it was the only thing he ever wanted to do." John pointed at a photo just past Chase's shoulder. "That one was taken at Las Vegas."

Quinn thought Sean McCloud looked thinner, older and more cynical in this photo than the last. He stood with two other men, the reins of a horse in his hand, against a backdrop of penned steers and bulls.

"That was taken the last time I saw him," John continued. "He left for Idaho from Vegas. Our grandfather told Sean if he didn't come home and take over his responsibilities at the ranch, he was done with him." The older man's face held regret. "I should have done a better job of keeping track of him. I tried to reach him when Granddad fell ill, but his contact numbers no longer worked and no one knew where he'd gone."

"So he didn't have a chance to make peace with his grandfather before he died?" Quinn asked, although he knew the answer. He wanted John to keep talking. Somehow, hearing someone who'd known his father made Sean McCloud seem more real, less like fiction.

"No." John shook his head. "When I couldn't find him, Dad and I hired detectives. Months after Granddad passed away, the detectives finally tracked Sean to Texas and then Mexico, but it was too late. Sean died when a bull gored him at a rodeo in southern Mexico. Friends of Sean's said he'd had a wife and child, but the detectives reached a dead end. They couldn't find any records of a marriage or birth in either Mexico City or Texas."

"So the friends were wrong," Quinn commented. "No wife, no kid. He died alone."

"We didn't find a record of a wife or child," John corrected him. "That doesn't mean Sean didn't have a family."

"No?" Quinn lifted an eyebrow at the conviction in the older man's voice.

"I've always believed Sean had a child. He called a friend in Texas before he died and told him he'd just found out he was going to be a daddy."

"Do you believe the friend?"

"The investigator did," John said. "Which is why I went to Texas and talked to the man myself." He paused, staring broodingly into the dark brew in his cup. "But Sean died before he had a chance to talk to the friend again."

"Maybe Sean was wrong."

"My gut tells me Sean was right," John said quietly. "And when we brought Sean's bones home and buried him in the cemetery at Wolf Creek, I swore I'd never stop looking."

"Have you still got an open case?" Quinn asked, surprised.

"I still have an agency on retainer, but beyond touching base with us, maybe once a year, there's not much they can do."

Quinn studied the man across the table. His chin was firm with resolve, his eyes clear and direct. "I've heard of homicide cold cases being worked by the cops for decades, but I don't think I've ever known a civilian to keep a missing person case active for this long."

"We'll never stop looking." John glanced at Chase. "When my father died, his will split his estate between me and Sean. I was the executor and although Sean died and I was legally his sole known heir, I kept his inheritance from Dad separate from mine. My family has worked the land and invested the money, but it's always been kept separate. When we find Sean's child, he or she will inherit all of Sean's share."

Quinn stared at John, unable to take in what he'd just heard. He flicked a sidelong glance at Chase, who confirmed his father's words with a brief nod.

"But you're not even sure there is a child."

"I don't have any proof that would hold up in court," John agreed with a shrug. "Just a gut feeling."

"And Dad's gut is never wrong," Chase said easily, a smile lighting his eyes.

A neighbor of the McClouds' stopped by the booth, interrupting the discussion, and within a half hour Quinn was on his way home. John and Chase hadn't returned to the topic of Sean McCloud and Quinn was just as glad. He was having trouble getting his head around a family so loyal to a brother and uncle that they'd hold an inheritance for a child they weren't even sure had been born.

Even more mind-blowing was that the child was Quinn.

All he had to do was step forward, show John a copy

of his original birth certificate and he'd instantly become a rich man.

The prospect was tempting. His bank account was comfortable, but he wasn't exactly Beverly Hills rich.

And he liked his life just fine the way it was. He'd purposely never owned anything he cared about that wouldn't fit in his truck and couldn't be packed to travel on a moment's notice. The one big exception to his rule was Buddy—adopting the yellow Lab was the biggest commitment he'd ever made to a home and hearth.

From what he'd observed of the McClouds, the concept of family connections and wealth carried a whole boatload of ties, obligations and complications.

Deciding whether to tell John McCloud that he was Sean's son was something he'd have to think about he decided as he parked at the apartment. He headed up the stairs to shower, change clothes and collect Buddy before heading back to the office.

Chapter Nine

"Hey, Quinn, catch!"

He looked up from the clock pieces on the table just in time to snag an airborne soft dog toy. Tansy laughed and clapped her hands when Buddy leaped and missed it.

"No throwing things in the parlor, Tansy." Abigail's stern reminder lost much of its impact when she laughed and rubbed Buddy's ears. "How's it going with the clock?"

Quinn shrugged, distracted by the gleam of lamplight in the silky fall of her hair. "I might need to order some parts, but cleaning the gears will probably fix it."

"That's great news." Abigail left Buddy to play with Tansy on the red-and-cream carpet and joined Quinn.

She touched a few of the gears spread across the butcher paper covering the tabletop, then stroked her hand over the curved top of the old mantel clock's walnut casing. "I confess, I miss the chimes going off every hour. It's odd but over the years I've grown so used to the sound that since it stopped, the silence feels odd."

"Just goes to prove that a person can get used to anything," he commented.

Color moved up her throat, turning her cheeks pink and Quinn realized he was staring. Again.

"Sorry." He trailed his fingertips over her wrist, giving her hand a brief squeeze before reluctantly releasing her. "I'm trying to keep my hands off you but I never promised not to look."

Her eyes darkened, her lips parting.

Before she could respond, Quinn's cell phone went off. He flipped it open, frowned at the number.

"Quinn here. What's up?"

Abigail lifted her hair off her neck in a vain effort to cool the flush of heat his gaze and touch had caused. As she watched him listen to the caller, his eyes went flat, losing the warmth they'd held only a second before.

"I'm on my way." He closed the phone and stood, catching his jacket off the back of the chair as he slid the phone into his jeans pocket. "I have to go to work. Can Buddy stay here?"

"Of course. We'd love to have him. Be careful," she murmured.

"I always am." He cupped her cheek, smoothed his thumb over her lower lip.

She was sure he meant to kiss her. But then he glanced at the child and dog on the carpet and his hand left her face.

"Tell Elizabeth I'll be back to finish the clock."

"I will," she murmured. She caught his arm as he turned away. "Be safe, Quinn."

His face softened. "Don't worry, Abby."

And he was gone. She heard his footfalls down the hall, his deep voice as he murmured something to Natasha in the kitchen and the closing of the back door as he left the house.

Outside, Quinn backed his truck out of the alley and turned onto the street before he hit Redial on his phone.

"Yeah, boss." Karl's response was instant.

"Where are you?"

"Parked behind the minimart, a half block east of the auction barn."

"I'll be there in five. Are the suspects still inside the barn?"

"Yeah. I've got a good view of the office door from my position."

"Call the state troopers. Tell them we need backup. And request they set up roadblocks on every road out of town. If the suspects slip past us, I want them stopped."

"Will do."

Quinn rang off. He turned left on Sheridan Street and flicked off his lights. Halfway down the block, a black four-wheel-drive pickup pulled in behind him, also running without lights.

"What the hell?" he muttered. He braked and made a fast turn at an intersection. When the truck followed him through the turn, Quinn saw the McCloud Ranch logo on the door panel.

He didn't know why the truck was following him, but at least he didn't have to worry about the driver being one of the bad guys.

Quinn spun the wheel and returned to Sheridan Street. A minute later, he turned down the alley running behind the minimart and entered the back parking lot. The cruiser was backed into a parking space, nose out, lights off. Quinn backed in next to it and got out. The black pickup followed and when the doors opened, no interior lights flicked on.

Karl joined Quinn, both watching as Luke McCloud and Zach Kerrigan stepped out of the black truck.

"Hey, Quinn." Luke's deep voice rang with interest. "What's up?"

"Police business—and you're both civilians. Go home." Quinn's voice wasn't polite, nor was it hostile. He didn't have time to waste.

"We're civilians with guns and experience in military ops," Zach said, just as brusquely. "We've got a police scanner in the truck, so we know there's a break-in at the barn." He looked from Quinn to Karl; then his hard gaze met Quinn's once more. "We're backup."

"I got that same song and dance from Chase," Quinn told him. "But at least he was backup for a bar fight. This is a break-in. There might be shots fired."

"No problem."

"You're carrying?" Quinn asked.

Luke and Zach both flipped open their jackets, revealing handguns.

"Hell," Quinn said quietly. "Are all you McClouds crazy?"

"They're good, Quinn," Karl said quietly. "Solid." He jerked a thumb over his shoulder in the direction of the barn. "And I saw at least six men go through that door."

"All right, you're in," Quinn said with quick decision. "But you're backup, not primary, understand?"

"Got it," Luke said tersely.

"I've walked through the barn with Walt and know the basics, but you might know any details he forgot to mention," Quinn told the other three. "Tell me the layout and the best way in."

Karl gave him a brief outline. "That's about it. The office has only one way in from the outside but there's a door that lets Walt go through to the barn's interior without going back outside." He looked at Luke and Zach. "Did I miss anything?"

"I think you covered the basics," Luke said.

"Except I'm not sure about the number of doors into the barn from outside," Zach said, frowning. "There might be a few more from the stalls along the backside.

I don't remember exactly how many private horse stalls there are back there."

Quinn swore. "So we've got a building with multiple entries and only four of us to cover them."

"That's about it."

Abby was right, Quinn though with sudden insight. *Having family can be a good thing.* And being connected to men like Luke and Chase McCloud felt damn good right now.

It was nearly ten o'clock before Quinn finished writing reports at the sheriff's office and returned home. The Foster house blazed with light, so instead of going to his apartment, he climbed the porch steps and knocked.

Abby answered the door, her face lighting when she saw him.

"Come in, come in." She caught his jacket sleeve and tugged him inside the foyer, closing the door quietly before going up on her toes to wrap her arms around him as she pressed her mouth to his.

When she eased back and grinned up at him, he shook his head in an attempt to clear the fog of arousal "Wow. Now that's the way a man ought to be welcomed home," he told her. "What's the occasion?"

"I'm just happy to see you. Also," she paused dramatically. "Tansy's father's here!"

"You're kidding." Quinn could only stare at her in surprise.

"Not kidding. He arrived an hour ago. It seems the military had trouble reaching him in Afghanistan but the moment he learned what happened to his mother-in-law, he flew home. He said he had a few bad moments when he couldn't find Tansy but then the neighbor—whose daughter brought Tansy to us—told him what happened. He drove straight here." Her eyes went misty. "You should have seen Tansy's face when she saw him."

Quinn brushed the tip of his forefinger over her lashes; they came away damp. "Kind of like your face now?"

"Maybe." She smiled at him. "Come in and meet him."

She caught his hand and drew him into the living room. A tall man in a black T-shirt and jeans, his dark hair clipped short in a military buzz cut, was seated on the sofa.

Abigail quickly completed introductions and Quinn settled into the wingback chair while she perched on the padded arm.

Tansy was curled up on her father's lap, an afghan tucked around her, her eyes sleepy, both hands curled around Joseph's much bigger hand. His arm curved protectively around her, holding her close.

"I can only apologize for the confusion, Elizabeth," he said, continuing the conversation interrupted by Quinn's arrival. "When my mother-in-law was hospitalized and couldn't care for Tansy, it was her wish to have Tansy brought here. I thought it was the perfect solution." He grinned at Elizabeth. "I've never forgotten those cookies you gave me during those long hours

I spent sweeping the library floors and cleaning after school. I doubt Sheriff Adams knew what a favor he did me when he assigned me community service in your library after I broke the pharmacy window." His eyes softened. "Those were some of the best hours of my preteen years, before we moved away from Wolf Creek and went to Billings." He bent and brushed a kiss over the crown of Tansy's head.

"All's well that ends well," Natasha said. She nodded at Tansy. "I think it's time the little one is in bed."

Tansy stirred, protesting. "No, don't wanna go to bed."

"Maybe we all should head for bed," Elizabeth said. "It's been a long, exciting evening and it's late." She stood. "I've made up the guest room next to Tansy's for you, Joseph. She'll sleep better if you're close." She began to clear the table; Abigail and Quinn joined her.

"Can Buddy stay with me tonight?" Tansy asked.

Quinn lifted a brow and Elizabeth nodded. "All right," he conceded. "But he has to come home in the morning, okay?"

"'Kay."

Joseph carried Tansy, following Natasha upstairs. Buddy trotted at their heels.

"I'm off to bed, too." Elizabeth paused in the doorway. "Good night, Quinn."

"Sleep well, Elizabeth."

Quinn and Abigail were left alone in the kitchen.

"It's lovely to see her so happy, isn't it?" Abigail said.

"Who? Elizabeth?"

"No, Tansy—with her father."

"Oh. Yeah." He searched her face, saw the soft droop of her mouth, the shadows in her eyes. "Come with me."

"Where?"

"To my apartment." He threaded his fingers through hers and pulled her close, bending to brush her mouth with his.

She nodded and he led her out of the house, half jogging across the back lawn, the air cold against their faces.

Quinn unlocked the door and pushed it open, tugging Abigail with him over the threshold. The only light in the apartment came from the streetlights outside and the small lamp next to the stove on the kitchen counter. Quinn pushed the door shut and pulled Abigail into his arms.

She buried her face against his throat and wrapped her arms around him, her hands fisting in the back of his T-shirt.

Abby pressed against him, his heartbeat thudding, solid and sure, beneath her ear. "I was wrong," she murmured, burrowing closer.

"About what?" His hands smoothed over her back.

"I thought if I didn't admit I love you, you couldn't break my heart." She lifted her head, searching his face. "I was devastated when my husband died, didn't think I'd ever smile again. I didn't want to love anyone again."

"Oh, honey." His thumbs smoothed over her cheeks

and Abby realized she was crying. He wiped the tears away and cradled her face in his hands. "I'm not going to break your heart. I'm not going to die."

"Manny never thought he'd leave me, either, Quinn."

He brushed her mouth with his. "I'm not addicted to danger. I'm always careful and I know what I'm doing. For me, it's just a job."

She would have protested, not quite convinced, but his lips brushed hers again and the kiss eased from comfort and reassurance into heat that singed her body.

He swung her off her feet and she gasped, catching his shoulders. "What are you doing?"

"Taking you to bed." He strode into the bedroom and set her on her feet, catching the hem of her shirt to pull it up and off over her head. She emerged smiling, her hair tousled from the swift tug of her shirt over it.

Quinn stroked his palm over her bare shoulder, slipping one finger beneath the strap of her black lace bra, then tracing it downward until his thumb could smooth over the upper swell of her breast.

Abigail caught her breath, sighing as he cupped her breasts in his palms and bent his head to kiss the skin just above the black lace.

"Quinn." She slid her fingers into hair, holding on as he released her bra hooks and the lace fell away. Her head fell back, her throat arching, and Quinn wrapped her close, his mouth finding the thunder of her pulse at the base of her throat.

His mouth took hers and she twisted against him, desperately trying to get closer. He tore his mouth from hers and stepped back to yank his T-shirt off over his head and rip open the buttons on his jeans. All modesty forgotten in the need to feel him against her, skin against skin, Abigail shrugged her shoulders and let her bra drop to the floor. She unzipped and pushed off her slacks and the bikini panties she wore underneath, toed off her shoes and climbed onto the bed, shifting back to let Quinn sit. He pulled off one boot and bent to remove the other.

Impatient to feel him against her, Abigail wrapped her arms around his shoulders, stroked her hands over the muscles of his chest and pressed her bare torso against the supple, heated warmth of his back. Quinn groaned and half turned, wrapped a hand around the back of her neck, and pulled her forward to meet his mouth. Hot and carnal, his kiss melted her bones.

He shuddered, released her and finished pulling off his second boot. Then he stood, shucking off jeans and boxers in one downward shove, before he stepped out of them and rolled on protection. Abigail wrapped her arms around his neck and tugged him forward, urging him down on top of her, and his weight settled over her, her hips cradling the hard thrust of his.

Abigail was burning up and she didn't protest when he nudged her knees apart and wedged between them. The first blunt brush of him between her legs had her arching off the sheets, trying to get closer, faster. Quinn stroked her, soothed her, then flexed his hips and pushed forward, joining them.

She struggled to adjust to the sudden intrusion and he went still, giving her time. His mouth covered hers, seducing her until she relaxed beneath him and he slid home, pulling almost out before thrusting forward again. Abigail groaned, twisting beneath him until she caught his rhythm, the tension ratcheting between them until the world exploded.

Long moments later, Abigail curled against his side, her arm across his chest, her knee riding his thigh and her head on his shoulder.

"Do you think Joseph will go back to Billings to live?"

"I don't know," Quinn said, his deep voice rumbling just above her. "I suppose so."

"I wish they'd stay in Wolf Creek. I know I should be happy Tansy's father is here with her," she said, her voice catching. "And I am—but I've grown used to having her in the house. I'll miss her so much."

Quinn pressed a kiss to her temple, cuddling her closer. "I know, honey. I was afraid this would happen."

"Was it wrong for me to grow attached to her?"

"No, Abby. You did a good thing. She needed you and thank God, you were there. What if she'd been left with someone who hadn't been kind to her, who hadn't cared?" he pointed out.

She pressed her face against his throat and though

her deep shuddering sobs slowed, he knew the dampness on his skin was her tears. Her heart was breaking. Quinn felt a growing ache in his own chest at her distress.

"Honey, you can't let this upset you so much," he said gently, trying to ease her pain.

"I want a child of my own, Quinn," she whispered, leaning back to look up at him. Damp streaks marked the path of tears down her cheeks, her eyes shadowed.

"I'll give you babies, Abigail." The words were out before he knew he was going to say them, but once they were, he knew they were right. This is what he wanted. "Marry me."

She searched his face, her mouth soft, vulnerable, her eyes naked with longing. "I wouldn't marry you just to have a child," she whispered.

"Then marry me because I love you and a child will be a bonus," he said, his voice husky in the quiet room.

She smiled, her lips trembling. "Are you offering me a deal?"

"Whatever it takes to get you to say yes."

She cupped his face in her palms and brushed her lips over his before she pulled back a few inches to look into his eyes. "I love you, too, Quinn. And I'd marry you even without children." Her words were a solemn vow.

Abigail lost track of the number of times they made love. The dark night shaded to gray on the eastern horizon before they finally fell asleep.

She woke to the smell of coffee. The mattress dipped beside her and warm lips nuzzled her throat.

"Wake up, Abby."

She slitted open one eye and glared at him. "What time is it?" her voice scratched.

"Just after seven." Quinn sat up and grinned down at her. "I brought you coffee."

She pushed up, sitting against the headboard, scowling at his cheerful face.

He picked up the mug and handed it to her, his gray eyes full of amusement.

Fortunately for Quinn, he wisely let her drink half the mug's liquid before he spoke again. "Are you always this chirpy when you wake up?"

"I'm never chirpy," she told him. "And definitely not in the morning. But——" she smiled sunnily and leaned forward to brush her fingers through the soft, thick black hair at his temple "——I could be very, very grateful to a man who brought me coffee every morning."

"Hmm." Quinn obeyed the tug of her fingers and kissed her.

"What a lovely way to wake up," Abigail sighed when he lifted his head. "Will you promise to bring me coffee every morning and wake me with kisses?"

"Sure," Quinn agreed. "I'll even throw in some foreplay and if you're fast, we can add sex to the mix."

She frowned at him but couldn't keep a smile from ruining the effect. "You're incorrigible."

"And insatiable, evidently, when it comes to you."

"I have to jump in the shower," she told him. "Or I'll be late for work."

"I'll join you," he said promptly.

"You're already dressed," she pointed out.

"I can be naked in two seconds," he shot back.

She rolled her eyes at him and pushed at his chest. He obliged by moving back, sprawling across the foot of the bed as she caught up her clothes off a nearby chair and walked naked into the bathroom.

"Nice—" he began. She shot him a glare over her shoulder. "View," he finished.

Abigail slammed the door and heard his laughter through the panels.

She smiled, located a towel and stepped into the shower, thinking about all they'd said the night before— and all they hadn't talked about.

They hadn't discussed where they'd live. She wondered if he'd mind staying in the apartment for a while, just until they found a house. There was a lovely old home for sale only two blocks away, but she didn't know the price and, she suddenly realized, she had no idea what Quinn could afford.

Nor did she know if he'd considered accepting the sheriff's position permanently.

She hurriedly rinsed and stepped out of the shower to dry off. Before they left for work, she wanted to ask him a few questions so she could begin to make plans.

Happiness fizzed as she brushed her teeth and pulled on her clothes.

Five minutes later, happiness was a dim memory.

They stood in the small kitchen, facing each other with only a few feet between them, but Abigail felt as if those inches were the Grand Canyon.

"But of course I assumed we'd live here." She lifted her hand, gestured, then lowered it, all while staring at him, uncomprehending.

"If we make Wolf Creek our base, I won't get to see you as often," he said. "I need to be in Seattle. There's an international airport less than forty-five minutes from my apartment. And Ren's main offices are there."

"Are you going to keep working for Ren Colter?" Abby asked, trying to get her mind around what he was telling her.

"Of course. It's my job, Abby." He took her hand, threading his fingers through hers. "You didn't think we'd live here, did you?"

"Yes, I did."

"Abby," he said quietly. "Wolf Creek is a nice town. The people are great. But I can't imagine spending my life here. It's too small and too quiet—and there's no work here for me."

"The sheriff's job is still open," she pointed out. But she knew what he'd say before he shook his head.

"I can't settle here, Abby."

"And I can't leave to follow you around the world, Quinn."

"You don't have to follow me. Seattle's a great city. We can make our home base there, buy a house, raise our kids there."

She shook her head, tears trickling down her cheeks, scratching in the back of her throat. "It doesn't matter how nice the city is, Quinn, I'd still be waiting, alone or with our children, for a call from Ren telling me that this time you won't be coming home. I can't do it. I'm not strong enough."

"You won't come with me." His voice was rough with emotion.

"I love you, Quinn. Too much to wait at home, wondering if you'll return upright or in a body bag."

His gaze searched hers, dark with emotion and pain. Then he reached out and pulled her close, his face buried in her hair as he breathed her in. Her tears dampened his throat and shirt collar.

Three days later, Quinn drove to the McCloud ranch and located John in the machine shop. After saying hello, he wasted no time getting to the purpose of his visit.

Quinn looked at John's open, friendly expression. "There's something I'd like to talk to you about."

"Sure." John tucked his hands into his pants pockets, clearly waiting for Quinn to speak.

"I meant to tell you this earlier but between taking

over the sheriff's office and helping Abigail—" he shrugged "—I've been a little short of time."

John waited, his expression curious but patient.

Quinn ran his palm over his hair, then shoved his hands into the pockets of his jeans. "Remember when your wife asked me about my name—and whether I was related to you?"

John nodded. "Yeah, I remember. You said you were adopted."

"That's right. I didn't lie about being adopted, but I didn't exactly tell you the whole truth. My adoptive father's last name was Kennedy. My biological father's name was McCloud—Sean McCloud."

John's eyes widened, his expression stunned. "You're Sean's boy?"

"I never knew him. He died before I was born. And you should know he never married my mother— I'm illegitimate."

"Hell," John waved his hand dismissively. "I don't care if they didn't get married, doesn't change a thing as far as I'm concerned." His eyes narrowed in thought. "But that might explain why the investigators couldn't find you and your mother. If they never were married, there wouldn't have been any records connected to Sean and your birth."

"My mother listed Sean McCloud on my birth certificate but I was born in a little town in Texas. She said she was following the rodeo circuit and I was born early.

Then she went home and married my stepfather a couple of years later. I always knew I was adopted, but didn't know my father's name until I moved the court to allow access to my file when I was eighteen."

"Why did you do that?"

Quinn shrugged. "Curiosity, I guess. I never got along with my stepfather. I decided to change my name to one that belonged to me so I went looking for my biological father's information."

"You've known Chase for a few years. Does he know?"

"No, I didn't tell him. Didn't see the point."

"I'm glad you told me. And Margaret will be happy to learn she was right."

"I'm sorry?"

John chuckled. "After you visited us at the house that first time, she told me she had a gut feeling you were connected to the rest of us McClouds. Women's intuition, she said. Anyway, she was right." His eyes glowed with satisfaction. "And I'm glad. You're a fine addition to the family, Quinn. Your dad would be proud."

"I'm not expecting anything from this," Quinn told him, wanting to set the record straight.

"Sure, sure son," John said. "But like I told you that day at breakfast, I always knew deep in my gut that Sean's kid was out there, somewhere. And as long as I lived, I never would have stopped looking. The family has kept Sean's inheritance safe and cared for—and it's yours."

"I can't accept it." Quinn said bluntly.

"Then I'll hold it for your children."

Quinn's gaze locked with his. Neither man backed down. A long moment later, a reluctant grin tugged at Quinn's lips. "You're a stubborn man, John McCloud."

An answering grin lifted the corner of the older man's mouth. "Takes one to know one, Quinn." He lifted an eyebrow. "I'll make you a deal."

"What's that?" Quinn asked warily.

"You submit to DNA testing. If the test proves you're my nephew, you'll accept his legacy. If not, you're off the hook but we stay friends. Deal?"

Quinn eyed him. "Either way, you win."

"Son," John said with a slow amused drawl. "I haven't lived this long or got this rich because I made deals I think I'll lose."

Quinn laughed. "All right, you win." He held out his hand and the two clasped hands.

"Welcome to the family."

"We have to have a DNA test first," Quinn cautioned him.

Again, John waved a hand dismissively. "A mere formality. My gut tells me you're Sean's boy. Your father's legacy to you has been waiting for more than thirty-plus years. It can wait a little longer for you to accept it." He threw an arm around Quinn's shoulders in a quick, hard hug.

Two days later, Quinn said goodbye and left Montana for a new assignment with Colter Investigations.

Chapter Ten

The days passed slowly, piling up into weeks. The air turned colder and snow fell on Wolf Creek. Abigail now wore heavier boots, gloves, hat and her warmer wool coat when she walked to work in the mornings.

The town gossip hotline was abuzz with the rumor that the middle-aged man hired by the town council to fill the sheriff's slot wasn't happy. Rumor had it he'd been offered a job in Portland, Oregon, where the weather was milder and his wife would be closer to the urban shopping she apparently enjoyed.

Abigail heard the rumors but was uncharacteristically quiet on that front.

She was relieved when Elizabeth and Natasha seemed to understand that she didn't want to talk about Quinn. She thought about him constantly, though, and his absence left an ever-present ache in her heart.

She'd been right to worry that falling in love with Quinn would bring pain, she thought as she stood in the kitchen drinking her morning coffee. The familiar routine that had once soothed her now seemed to leave her walking through the hours feeling strangely disconnected.

A door slammed outside, breaking the quiet in the big kitchen. Abigail looked out the window at the backyard and saw Tansy clattering down the steps from the apartment over the garage, followed by her father. She reached the bottom and turned to look up at him, laughing as he took her hand. The two walked across the snow-covered backyard on their way to Abigail's back door, Tansy bouncing along beside her tall father.

The one bright spot in all of this, Abigail reflected as she crossed the kitchen and porch to open the door for the two, was that Tansy was still in their lives. Joseph had accepted an offer with the highway patrol office in Wolf Creek. The new job allowed him to work a day shift, which meant he could spend more time with his daughter. He'd moved Tansy's grandmother into Wolf Creek Convalescent Center, rented the empty apartment over the Fosters' garage and each morning before he left for work at his office across town, he delivered Tansy to Abigail.

"Good morning." Abigail smiled at the two as they reached the porch, knocking the snow from their boots on the step before they entered.

"Hi, Abigail," Tansy said brightly, her face wreathed in smiles. "Daddy says we can get a dog this weekend. If it's okay with you and Aunt Elizabeth and Aunt Natasha," she added when her dad tapped her shoulder.

"Well, I…" Abigail struggled with the sudden mental image of a big yellow Lab, loping along beside Quinn, rolling in the fall leaves with Tansy. But Tansy eyed her anxiously and Abigail forced herself to continue. "I think it's a great idea. Why don't you go check with Elizabeth and Natasha? They're in the parlor."

"Yay!" Tansy bent to tug off her boots, leaving them on the heavy rug in the porch before dashing down the hallway.

Joseph shook his head and gave Abigail a wry look. "She's been hassling me to get a dog for weeks. Are you sure you don't mind?"

"I like dogs," Abigail told him.

He followed her into the kitchen, unzipped his jacket and took the cup of coffee she handed him. "I thought she'd be happy with a little dog, but she insists it has to be a big one, preferably a Labrador or a Great Dane."

Abigail's eyes widened. "A Great Dane? Aren't they as big as small ponies?"

"That's my understanding." He grinned when she

rolled her eyes. "So I'm guessing that's a 'no' on the pony-size dog?"

"Labrador retrievers are nice," she said weakly, still occupied with the ramifications of having a Great Dane romping about in the yard and flower beds.

"We'll see what the aunts have to say." He pushed back his sleeve. "Gotta run or I'll be late." He strode down the hall to say goodbye to his daughter. When he reappeared, his mouth was curved in a bemused smile. "Those three are in there discussing the size of possible dogs for Tansy and Elizabeth has a coffee-table book with full-color pictures."

Abigail laughed. "I think you've been outmaneuvered, Joseph."

"I think you're right." He headed for the door. "I'll be by to pick up Tansy around five-thirty. Thanks again for letting her stay here before and after school, Abigail."

"It's our pleasure," she assured him. "We've grown so used to having her with us that life would be unbearably dull if we didn't get to see her every day. So you're actually doing us a favor."

He grinned at her. "I'll remind you of those words when she gets into trouble with the new dog."

Abigail laughed and waved him off. Joseph was a nice man, she thought as she saw his truck drive down the alley and into the street. It was really too bad that she felt none of the attraction that drew her to Quinn.

For what felt like the millionth time, she pondered

the impasse between them. She loved him. He loved her. But he couldn't stay in Wolf Creek and live a quiet life.

So, could she change? Could she leave Wolf Creek, give up the life she loved to travel from place to place with Quinn? In fact, she wasn't sure his job would let her travel with him. Once they had children, traveling wouldn't have been possible, but what about before?

Abigail stared unseeingly out the window, pondering the knotty question. Unfortunately, she arrived at the same answer that always ended her contemplation of the situation. She didn't think she could bear worrying over his being shot on assignment, nor enduring the long hours spent waiting and wondering if he were dead or alive.

Much as she wanted Quinn, she was convinced that eventually the life he lived would make her hate the situation, and gradually destroy their love.

Somehow, the thought of him dying in a strange city was harder to accept than the possibility that his life might be—would surely be—endangered to a certain extent had he stayed in Wolf Creek as sheriff. Maybe it was because this was home and she knew its people so she felt he was safer here? Abby didn't know why, but she wasn't as tortured by the thought of Quinn being a sheriff as she was knowing he was far away, putting his life on the line for a Colter Agency client.

Regardless of the reasons, however, hard as she tried, she could see no solution. She had to get on with her life.

She sighed, turning away from the counter to tuck coffee cups into the dishwasher. Determinedly, she pinned a smile on her face and went into the parlor to join the discussion about Tansy's new dog.

Thanksgiving came and went. The week after a turkey dinner shared with Tansy, Joseph, Abigail's aunts and several of their friends, Abigail geared up for Christmas at the library.

The old building lent itself beautifully to Christmas decorations. Evergreen wreaths tied with red velvet bows glowed with bright color against the pristine white columns of the exterior. Strings of twinkling lights were entwined with evergreen garlands that draped the entry lintel and trailed down the outside of the doorjamb. Each time Abigail walked through the doorway, she breathed in the fragrant evergreen scent of the season.

Inside, the dark oak interior glowed with holiday colors. Three evergreen wreaths were hung just below the oak countertop, linked together by lengths of bright red wooden craftsmen beads. Elderly Owen Johnson had carved and strung the beads a half century before with his father and the beautiful strings had figured prominently in the library's holiday decorations ever since. Now ninety-two, he beamed with pride each time he entered the building during the holidays.

Wooden nutcrackers in the shape of soldiers stood with hand-carved Santa Clauses on the top shelves in the children's section, guarding a selection of Christmas-themed hardcover books. The bright wooden toys and the colorful covers of the books were festive and enticing.

At 10:30 a.m., Abigail wrestled the tall maintenance ladder from the storage room at the back of the library out into the main room, centering it under the main light fixture between the door and the stacks, just past the checkout counter.

"You're not going to hang the garlands up there yourself, are you, Abby?" Linda Graves appeared from an aisle of bookcases, a stack of books in her arms. She eyed the ladder with concern.

"I've done it before," Abigail said with a shrug. "Come to think of it, I think I've always been the one to string the garlands around the lights. Mostly because I'm too impatient to wait for one of the weekend volunteers to do it."

"Be careful," Linda cautioned as Abigail draped the short lengths of garland over the short platform on the back of the ladder, carefully set a cardboard box of glass Christmas balls atop the greenery and started up the rungs.

"Seriously," she told Linda, "don't worry. I'm fine. Go back to filing."

But Linda remained where she was, watching with a worried frown while Abigail climbed the ladder and expertly draped evergreens and clipped red and gold glass balls around the metal framework of the chandelier. The glass balls dangled from the hooks, catching and reflecting red and gold prisms of light across the room.

It wasn't until Abigail was safely back on the polished oak flooring that the other woman heaved a sigh of relief.

"Okay, I'll go back to filing books. You've clearly got this handled." She laughed when Abigail rolled her eyes at her. Linda waggled her fingers in response and disappeared down an aisle. The ensuing thud of books sliding onto shelves told Abigail the other woman had gone back to work.

Abigail dragged the ladder several feet to the next light and climbed up to drape more garland. She was perched on the ladder when the outer door opened, ushering a gust of snow and cold air into the warm interior. The chilled air made a direct hit on Abigail.

She shivered and looked over her shoulder to ask the patron to hurry and close the door. She froze. Her heart felt as if it had stopped beating and her vocal cords refused to work.

Quinn strode across the oak floor toward her. He wore boots, jeans and a thigh-length brown canvas coat lined in sheepskin. Snowflakes dusted his black hair. His skin was even more suntanned than when he'd left and faint lines fanned at the edges of his eyes as he frowned at her.

He was achingly familiar and dear. Absorbed with drinking in the sight of him, she couldn't summon her voice.

"What the hell are you doing up there?" he growled. His long legs ate up the distance from door to ladder.

His hands closed on her waist and he lifted her unceremoniously off the ladder.

She gasped, grabbing his shoulders to brace herself as her feet left the rung. The surprise unfroze her vocal cords. "Put me down," she demanded. Unfortunately, her voice trembled, undermining the authority in her command.

"Do I have to?" he asked, his face below hers.

If she said no, he'd kiss her. And she badly wanted him to. But Abigail had recovered from the shock of seeing him just enough to realize she had no idea why he was here. Until she did, it would be far wiser to keep him at a distance. Otherwise, the pain of his leaving would be fresh all over again.

So she didn't follow her heart, she did the smart thing. "Yes, you do."

He made a noise in his throat that sounded curiously like a growl before he walked to the counter and set her down on top of the polished oak.

"I meant put me on my feet—on the floor," she told him.

Her hands still rested on his shoulders and he didn't give her time to inch away from him. Instead, he nudged her knees apart, stepped between them and planted his hands palm down on the counter just behind her bottom.

"I don't want to give you time to think of all the reasons this won't work, Abigail." He leaned closer and kissed her.

His mouth was warm, seductive. He lifted his head, his lips leaving hers much too soon.

"I hate being away from you. Couldn't settle, couldn't focus on work. Maybe I could learn to live without you, but I don't want to." His hand cupped her cheek, his face softening. "I'm taking the sheriff's job permanently. Marry me, Abigail."

His thumb stroked over her lip and she tasted salt. She realized she was crying.

"Honey?" His deep voice roughened and a frown pulled down his brows. "Don't cry. If you don't want to marry me, I can accept that—for now. But I'm not going away this time. And I'll keep coming around until you give in."

She laughed, the sound watery. "You can't do that—it's harassment. You'd have to arrest yourself."

He looked baffled. "So…maybe we'll date?"

"No." She shook her head, slipping her arms around his neck until her fingers could thread into the silky black hair at his nape.

"No dating?"

"No." She lifted her legs, wrapped them around his waist and pulled him closer until he was fitted snugly against her. His eyes flared with heat. "No dating."

"So," he managed to get out. "What are we doing?"

"I've always wanted a Christmas wedding," she said dreamily, her lips finding the throb of his pulse at the base of his throat. Beneath her tongue, the pound of his pulse leaped.

"Are you going to stop teasing and say yes?" he growled, hands flexing against the curve of her bottom.

"Yes," she breathed against his throat. She tipped her head back and looked up into his face. "I will marry you, Quinn McCloud."

"Before Christmas," he demanded.

"Christmas Eve?"

"It's a date." His mouth took hers.

Abigail wrapped her arms and legs around him, reveling in the heat and power that surrounded her.

"Ahem. Abigail? Abigail?"

Someone called her name, louder, more insistently. She pulled away from Quinn and looked around, disoriented.

Linda stood near the door, her eyes twinkling with amusement. "Much as I hate to break this up, the pre-school class is a half block away."

"What?" Abigail was having difficulty focusing on what Linda was trying to tell her.

"Story hour—three- and four-year-olds? Twelve of them?" Linda prompted. "They're about to pour through the door and I'm thinking you might want to get down from the counter before they arrive…?"

"Oh." Abigail's face flushed with heat. She glanced at Quinn and found his eyes laughing at her. "Stop that—and let me down," she demanded, pushing at his chest.

"If I have to." He stepped back and lifted her easily off the counter.

She wobbled, her legs felt as if his kiss had melted her bones. Quinn steadied her, pulling her closer until her weight was supported against his hard body. She yearned, wishing they were alone.

Behind him, the door opened, letting in a rush of cold air accompanied by twelve chattering, laughing, very small boys and girls and their two teachers.

"I'll pick you up tonight when you close," Quinn murmured, stepping back, her hand in his. "And we can start planning our wedding."

Abigail nodded, not trusting her voice. Her gaze followed his broad back as he left the library, her heart bursting with a happiness she'd never known—until Quinn.

Christmas Eve arrived at last—and none too soon for Quinn's peace of mind. Although he knew he hadn't a single reason to worry, he couldn't get rid of the uneasy feeling that something might happen to stop the wedding. He was impatient to slip the ring on Abby's finger and hear the preacher declare them officially man and wife.

The big old church just off Main Street was decorated with poinsettias and draped with pine garlands. A huge fir tree stood to the left of the altar, gleaming with twinkling lights and glittering silver icicles.

Quinn stood at the back of the church, watching people arrive. He wasn't surprised that most of the population of Wolf Creek and many of the surrounding ranchers were in attendance. Abigail was well loved in the community and apparently her friends wanted to wish her well.

It occurred to him to wonder if he'd tap into that acceptance as her husband. Surprisingly, it felt good to hope so.

"Hey, Quinn." John McCloud entered the foyer from the church sanctuary.

"Good to see you, John. Where's Margaret?" Quinn asked when he realized John was alone.

"I left her sitting with the rest of the family. Thought I might catch you out here—wanted to tell you congratulations." The older man beamed at Quinn. "I always liked Abigail. You're getting a good woman and I think you just may be the one man who can handle her." He clapped a hand on Quinn's shoulder and laughed.

"She's a handful," Quinn agreed. "And that's only one of the things I like about her."

"I know what you mean. Margaret is a woman with strong opinions and we don't always agree, but I sure do admire a woman with a mind of her own."

"So do I."

"Are you ready to accept your father's legacy?" John asked.

"I'll think about it," Quinn said slowly.

"I'll talk to Abigail," John warned, grinning. "You'll accept—no more waiting."

"What's he waiting to accept?" Chase's voice interrupted. "I hope it's not Abigail."

"No." Quinn grinned. "I've waited as long as I plan to—we're getting married tonight if I have to kidnap her and fly her to Vegas."

"Very romantic," Raine McCloud commented dryly. "I wouldn't let Abigail hear you say that—not after all the work that's gone into this wedding."

"Just covering all the bases, Raine," Quinn drawled. "And making sure Abigail's my wife before Christmas Day."

Her face softened. "I'm sure she will be, Quinn."

The baby in her arms let out a muffled cry. All three of the men stiffened.

"Is she all right?" Chase asked, his arm over her shoulder as he bent protectively closer.

"Of course." Raine smiled indulgently at her husband. "I think she's hungry. If you gentlemen will excuse me, I'll go feed her." She looked at Chase. "I'll see you inside?"

"Absolutely." He tucked a strand of dark hair behind her ear. "I'll be the guy supporting Quinn at the altar."

Raine laughed and left them. The three men watched her thread her way through the crowd, stopped briefly several times by neighbor women who wanted to see her daughter. Then Raine disappeared down the hallway at the far side of the foyer.

Behind the second door of that same hallway, Abigail was putting the finishing touches on her bridal ensemble as Natasha fluffed out the fingertip netting of her veil. A longer underveil trailed down the back of the white gown and pooled on the floor at her feet.

"You look just like a princess." Tansy's awed voice

interrupted the women and Abigail looked over her shoulder.

Tansy, dressed in a matching white satin dress, held a basket of rose petals in white-gloved hands. Her brown hair was caught up in a pile of curls, her blue eyes pools of delight below the fringe of silky brown bangs.

"Thank you, sweetie." Abigail bent and gave her a quick hug. She felt a quick stab of regret that Tansy's mother couldn't be here to see her. She and Tansy had both lost their mother's when they were young, yet another reason she felt such kinship with her. She touched the gold locket on its gold chain around the little girl's neck. "How do you like your necklace?"

"I love it," Tansy said promptly. "Daddy says I can wear it only on special occasions, 'cause it's very special."

"Yes, it is." Abigail tapped the tip of her nose. "And it looks very elegant on you, don't you agree, Elizabeth?"

"Absolutely." Elizabeth nodded decisively, a fond smile curving her mouth. "And when you get married, it can be your 'something old.'"

Tansy frowned at her. "But it can't be something old. It's brand new."

"But by the time you grow up, fall in love and get married, it will be older," Natasha explained.

Tansy looked unconvinced. The women exchanged an amused smile.

The door rattled as someone rapped knuckles against the panels.

"Yes?" Elizabeth crossed the room and opened the door a small crack.

"The pastor said to tell you everyone's here and all is ready."

Elizabeth nodded, murmured something Abigail didn't catch and closed the door.

"It's time for us to take our seats, Abigail." She swept her into a hug. "Be happy, Abby-mine," she murmured.

"I love you, Elizabeth," Abigail told her, smiling into her aunt's misty eyes. Elizabeth sniffed, dabbed her eyes with her hanky and stepped back.

Then it was Natasha's turn. She wrapped Abigail in her arms, careful not to crush her gown or smudge her makeup. "You'll always be our girl, Abby."

"I know," Abigail managed to get out. Tears clogged her throat.

"Here now," Natasha said sternly. "None of that. You'll ruin your makeup and your mascara will run."

She handed Abigail a tissue before dabbing at her own eyes.

"Come on, Elizabeth, before I turn into a faucet."

The two hurried out, shooting one last smile at Abigail as they left.

Abigail drew in a deep breath and turned back to the mirror. The glass was taller than she was and reflected her from head to toe. She smoothed a palm over her abdomen, the white satin silky beneath her fingertips.

The dress had been her mother's, lovingly packed and stored in the attic of her aunt's house. Luckily, she and her mother were much the same size and very few alterations had been necessary to the simple white sheath. The scoop-neck bodice was overlaid with Irish lace, which also covered the snug long sleeves that came to a point just below her wrists. The bodice nipped in at the waist, the ankle-length skirt a narrow length of white satin, which would have been impossible to walk in were it not for the slit up the back.

Tansy appeared in the mirror, staring at her with awe and sheer pleasure. "You really do look like a princess," she said. "Or maybe a queen, even."

"Thank you, sweetie." Abigail tilted her head, listening. "I think the music has started. That's our cue. Are you ready?"

"Yes."

Abigail picked up the sheaf of red roses, baby's breath and white gardenias and took Tansy's hand. They left the room and entered the foyer, now empty of all but one tall, white-haired man.

"There you are." Walt Connors's voice was gruff. His eyes were suspiciously moist when the two females reached him. "You're a pair to draw to—prettiest two women I've seen all night."

Tansy tucked her chin and giggled. Abigail let go of her little hand and went up on tiptoe to brush a kiss against Walt's weathered cheek.

"And you're the handsomest man. Aren't we lucky, Tansy?"

Tansy nodded enthusiastically, setting the ribbons in her chignon flying.

"Harrumph." Walt cleared his throat and winked at them. "If you ladies are ready, I think there's a church full of people waiting for you to join them."

Tansy marched to the doorway and halted, waiting.

Walt held out his arm and Abigail tucked her hand into the curve of his elbow. Tansy looked over her shoulder and Abigail nodded.

The little girl faced forward and waved at someone inside. The music swelled as the organist began the wedding march. Tansy stepped through the doorway and started down the carpeted aisle.

Walt and Abigail walked the few feet to the doorway and halted, watching as Tansy made her way with measured steps toward the front of the church. Her gloved fingers plucked red rose petals from the basket and carefully tossed them with precision to first the right, then the left as she walked.

Walt bent toward Abigail. "You remember, honey, if that man of yours gives you any trouble, you just let me know. I'll take care of it."

Abigail met his gaze. "I love him, Walt. Quinn's a good man. But if either he or I ever need help, you're the first one I'll call."

Her words seemed to reassure him because his keen

gaze softened. "Good. That's what I thought, but I wanted to hear you say it." Shoulders squared, he nodded at the front of the church where Quinn waited. "We'd better get on with this, he's waiting."

Abigail looked down the aisle. Tansy had finished tossing rose petals and taken a seat in the front pew next to her father and Elizabeth.

"One, two," Walt counted under his breath. And just as they had during practice, they moved in easy rhythm down the aisle.

Quinn watched as they hesitated in the doorway. Walt bent to whisper to Abigail. She looked up and said something back.

Then they faced forward and started down the aisle.

Quinn had known the first time he saw Abigail that she was beautiful. He'd dreamed of her, fantasized about her, but tonight she was more than beautiful, she glowed. Happiness surrounded her, beamed from her face as she smiled.

He said a quick prayer of thanks that he was the one waiting for her and vowed he'd do his damnedest to never give her reason to regret marrying him.

She seemed to float down the red carpet on Walt's arm. Quinn knew there were other people in the church, but he saw only his bride as the two reached the steps to the altar and Walt placed Abigail's hand in his.

"Take good care of her, boy." Walt's voice was gruff with emotion.

"With my life, Walt," Quinn vowed, meeting the older man's gaze with his.

Walt nodded, one abrupt, brief movement of his head, and turned to take a seat alongside Natasha in the front pew.

Quinn and Abigail turned to climb the shallow steps and faced the preacher. He knew the service was meaningful and he tried to pay attention, tried to brand each word in his memory so he'd always remember. But the truth was, he wanted the pastor to fast-forward to the part where Abigail vowed to love him forever. He knew it was irrational to fear a last-minute interruption but couldn't erase the nagging concern.

At last, they faced the pastor to take their vows.

"Do you, Quinn Sean McCloud, take Abigail Marie Foster, as your wedded wife…"

Quinn waited impatiently for him to finish.

"I do." His deep voice rumbled and Abigail smiled mistily, her fingers trembling when he slid the matching platinum band on her finger, next to the square-cut diamond engagement ring. She'd insisted the stone was too large, but he'd overridden her protests. He wanted her to have visible proof of his vow to be steadfast and besides, her shocked delight when she opened the ring box had already told him she loved the ring.

"Do you, Abigail Marie Foster, take this man, Quinn Sean McCloud…"

He held out his hand, fingers rock steady as Abigail

slipped a heavy platinum band on the third finger of his left hand.

"You may kiss the bride."

"Yes," Quinn growled under his breath. Abigail's eyes widened, lightening with mirth before he swept her into his arms and kissed her.

When he let her up for air, the crowd in the pews was laughing and whistling. Quinn grinned and Abigail blushed.

"You're not embarrassed, are you?" he whispered in her ear, suddenly concerned.

She lifted her hand to his face, cupping his cheek.

"No, Quinn. I've waited a long time for this perfect moment. For the perfect man for me. I can't wait to start our life together—I love you."

And as she lifted onto her toes to reach him and her soft mouth molded to his, Quinn knew he'd waited for her forever, too. The future stretched before them, filled with bright promise.

* * * * *

*Celebrate 60 years of pure reading pleasure
with Harlequin®!
Just in time for the holidays,
Silhouette Special Edition® is proud to present
New York Times bestselling author
Kathleen Eagle's
ONE COWBOY, ONE CHRISTMAS*

Rodeo rider Zach Beaudry was a travelin' man—
until he broke down in middle-of-nowhere South
Dakota during a deep freeze. That's when an angel
came to his rescue....

"Don't die on me. Come on, Zel. You know how much I love you, girl. You're all I've got. Don't do this to me here. Not *now*."

But Zelda had quit on him, and Zach Beaudry had no one to blame but himself. He'd taken his sweet time hitting the road, and then miscalculated a short-cut. For all he knew he was a hundred miles from gas. But even if they were sitting next to a pump, the ten dollars he had in his pocket wouldn't get him out of South Dakota, which was not where he wanted to be right now. Not even his beloved pickup truck, Zelda, could get him much of anywhere on fumes. He was sitting out in the cold in the middle of nowhere. And getting colder.

He shifted the pickup into Neutral and pulled hard on the steering wheel, using the downhill slope to get her off the blacktop and into the roadside grass, where she shuddered to a standstill. He stroked the padded dash. "You'll be safe here."

But Zach would not. It was getting dark, and it was already too damn cold for his cowboy ass. Zach's battered body was a barometer, and he was feeling South Dakota, big time. He'd have given his right arm to be climbing into a hotel hot tub instead of a brutal blast of north wind. The right was his free arm anyway. Damn thing had lost altitude, touched some part of the bull and caused him a scoreless ride last time out.

It wasn't scoring him a ride this night, either. A carload of teenagers whizzed by, topping off the insult by laying on the horn as they passed him. It was at least twenty minutes before another vehicle came along. He stepped out and waved both arms this time, damn near getting himself killed. Whatever happened to *do unto others?* In places like this, decent people didn't leave each other stranded in the cold.

His face was feeling stiff, and he figured he'd better start walking before his toes went numb. He struck out for a distant yard light, the only sign of human habitation in sight. He couldn't tell how distant, but he knew he'd be hurting by the time he got there, and he was counting on some kindly old man to be answering the door. No shame among the lame.

It wasn't like Zach was fresh off the operating table—it had been a few months since his last round of repairs—but he hadn't given himself enough time. He'd lopped a couple of weeks off the near end of the doc's estimated recovery time, rigged up a brace, done some heavy-duty taping and climbed onto another bull. Hung in there for five seconds—four seconds past feeling the pop in his hip and three seconds short of the buzzer.

He could still feel the pain shooting down his leg with every step. Only this time he had to pick the damn thing up, swing it forward and drop it down again on his own.

Pride be damned, he just hoped *somebody* would be answering the door at the end of the road. The light in the front window was a good sign.

The four steps to the covered porch might as well have been four hundred, and he was looking to climb them with a lead weight chained to his left leg. His eyes were just as screwed up as his hip. Big black spots danced around with tiny red flashers, and he couldn't tell what was real and what wasn't. He stumbled over some shrubbery, steadied himself on the porch railing and peered between vertical slats.

There in the front window stood a spruce tree with a silver star affixed to the top. Zach was pretty sure the red sparks were all in his head, but the white lights twinkling by the hundreds throughout the huge tree, those were real. He wasn't too sure about the woman hanging the shiny balls. Most of her hair was caught up on her head and fastened in a curly clump, but the light captured by the escaped bits crowned her with a golden halo. Her face was a soft shadow, her body a willowy silhouette beneath a long white gown. If this was where the mind ran off to when cold started shutting down the rest of the body, then Zach's final worldly thought was, *This ain't such a bad way to go.*

If she would just turn to the window, he could die looking into the eyes of a Christmas angel.

* * * * *

Could this woman from Zach's past get the lonesome cowboy to come in from the cold...for good?

Look for
ONE COWBOY, ONE CHRISTMAS
by Kathleen Eagle
Available December 2009
from Silhouette Special Edition®

Copyright © 2009 by Kathleen Eagle

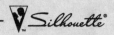

SPECIAL EDITION

We're spotlighting
a different series
every month throughout 2009
to celebrate our 60th anniversary.

This December, Silhouette Special Edition® brings you

NEW YORK TIMES BESTSELLING AUTHOR

KATHLEEN EAGLE

ONE COWBOY,
ONE CHRISTMAS

Available wherever books are sold.

Visit Silhouette Books at www.eHarlequin.com

SSE60BPA

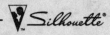
Silhouette®

SPECIAL EDITION

**FROM *NEW YORK TIMES* AND *USA TODAY*
BESTSELLING AUTHOR**

KATHLEEN EAGLE

ONE COWBOY,
One Christmas

When bull rider Zach Beaudry appeared
out of thin air on Ann Drexler's ranch,
she thought she was seeing a ghost of
Christmas past. And though Zach had
no memory of their night of passion years
ago, they were about to share a future
he would never forget.

*Available December 2009
wherever books are sold.*

SS65493

Visit Silhouette Books at www.eHarlequin.com

Silhouette® *Desire*

New York Times Bestselling Author

SUSAN MALLERY

HIGH-POWERED, HOT-BLOODED

Innocently caught up in a corporate scandal, schoolteacher Annie McCoy has no choice but to take the tempting deal offered by ruthless CEO Duncan Patrick. Six passionate months later, Annie realizes Duncan will move on, with or without her. Now all she has to do is convince him she is the one he really wants!

Available December 2009 wherever you buy books.

ALWAYS POWERFUL, PASSIONATE AND PROVOCATIVE

Visit Silhouette Books at www.eHarlequin.com

SD76981

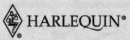

HARLEQUIN®

American ★ Romance®

A Cowboy Christmas
MARIN THOMAS

2 stories in 1!

The holidays are a rough time for widower
Logan Taylor and single dad Fletcher McFadden—
neither hunky cowboy has been lucky in love.
But Christmas is the season of miracles! Logan
meets his match in "A Christmas Baby," while
Fletcher gets a second chance at love in "Marry
Me, Cowboy." This year both cowboys are on
Santa's Nice list!

*Available December
wherever books are sold.*

"LOVE, HOME & HAPPINESS"

www.eHarlequin.com

HAR75292

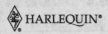
HARLEQUIN®

INTRIGUE®

FIRST NIGHT

BY

DEBRA
WEBB

To prove his innocence, talented artist
Brandon Thomas is in a race against time.
Caught up in a murder investigation,
he enlists Colby agent Merrilee Walters
to help catch the true killer. If they can survive
the first night, their growing attraction
may have a chance, as well.

Available in December wherever books are sold.

www.eHarlequin.com

HI69440

REQUEST YOUR FREE BOOKS!

2 FREE NOVELS PLUS 2 FREE GIFTS!

SPECIAL EDITION®

Life, Love and Family!

YES! Please send me 2 FREE Silhouette Special Edition® novels and my 2 FREE gifts (gifts are worth about $10). After receiving them, if I don't wish to receive any more books, I can return the shipping statement marked "cancel." If I don't cancel, I will receive 6 brand-new novels every month and be billed just $4.24 per book in the U.S. or $4.99 per book in Canada. That's a savings of at least 15% off the cover price! It's quite a bargain! Shipping and handling is just 50¢ per book.* I understand that accepting the 2 free books and gifts places me under no obligation to buy anything. I can always return a shipment and cancel at any time. Even if I never buy another book from Silhouette, the two free books and gifts are mine to keep forever.

235 SDN EYN4 335 SDN EYPG

Name	(PLEASE PRINT)
Address	Apt. #
City	State/Prov.	Zip/Postal Code

Signature (if under 18, a parent or guardian must sign)

Mail to the **Silhouette Reader Service:**
IN U.S.A.: P.O. Box 1867, Buffalo, NY 14240-1867
IN CANADA: P.O. Box 609, Fort Erie, Ontario L2A 5X3

Not valid to current subscribers of Silhouette Special Edition books.

Want to try two free books from another line?
Call 1-800-873-8635 or visit www.morefreebooks.com.

* Terms and prices subject to change without notice. Prices do not include applicable taxes. Sales tax applicable in N.Y. Canadian residents will be charged applicable provincial taxes and GST. Offer not valid in Quebec. This offer is limited to one order per household. All orders subject to approval. Credit or debit balances in a customer's account(s) may be offset by any other outstanding balance owed by or to the customer. Please allow 4 to 6 weeks for delivery. Offer available while quantities last.

Your Privacy: Silhouette is committed to protecting your privacy. Our Privacy Policy is available online at www.eHarlequin.com or upon request from the Reader Service. From time to time we make our lists of customers available to reputable third parties who may have a product or service of interest to you. If you would prefer we not share your name and address, please check here. ☐

SSE09R

HARLEQUIN® HISTORICAL:
Where love is timeless

**From chivalrous knights
to roguish rakes, look for the
variety Harlequin® Historical
has to offer every month.**

www.eHarlequin.com

HHBRANDINGBPA09

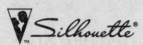

COMING NEXT MONTH
Available November 24, 2009

#2011 ONE COWBOY, ONE CHRISTMAS—Kathleen Eagle

When bull rider Zach Beaudry appeared out of thin air on Ann Drexler's ranch, she thought she was seeing a ghost of Christmas past. And though Zach had no memory of their night of passion years ago, they were about to share a future he would never forget.

#2012 CHRISTMAS AT BRAVO RIDGE—Christine Rimmer
Bravo Family Ties

Lovers turned best friends Matt Bravo and Corrine Lonnigan had been there, done that with each other, and had a beautiful daughter. But their affair was ancient history…until old flames reignited over the holidays—and Corrine made Matt a proud daddy yet again!

#2013 A COLD CREEK HOLIDAY—RaeAnne Thayne
The Cowboys of Cold Creek

Christmas had always made designer Emery Kendall sad. But this Cold Creek Christmas was different—she rediscovered her roots… and found the gift of true love with rancher Nate Cavazos, whose matchmaking nieces steered Emery and Nate to the mistletoe.

#2014 A NANNY UNDER THE MISTLETOE—
Teresa Southwick
The Nanny Network

Libby Bradford had nothing in common with playboy Jess Donnelly—except for their love of the very special little girl in Jess and Libby's care. But the more time Libby spent with her billionaire boss, the more the mistletoe beckoned….

#2015 A WEAVER HOLIDAY HOMECOMING—Allison Leigh
Men of the Double-C Ranch

Former agent Ryan Clay just wanted to forget his past. Then Dr. Mallory Keegan came to town—with the child he never knew he had. Soon, Ryan discovered the joy only a Christmas spent with the little girl—and her beautiful Aunt Mallory—could bring.

#2016 THE TEXAS TYCOON'S CHRISTMAS BABY—
Brenda Harlen
The Foleys and the McCords

When Penny McCord found out her lover Jason Foley was using her to get info about her family's jewelry-store empire, she was doubly devastated—for Penny was pregnant. Would a Christmas miracle reunite them…and reconcile their feuding families for good?

SSECNMBPA1109